Willem

THE WITCHES OF WIMBERLEY
BOOK 1

VICTORIA DANANN

PROLOGUE

IN THE YEAR 1838 in England, only a handful of high-waymen still practiced the highly romanticized profession of stand-and-deliver. Deck Durbin persevered, fancying himself smarter and faster than the arms of law enforcement who were determined to make the roads safe for noblemen, and their women, once and for all.

After a particularly successful haul on the old Roman road that ran south all the way to London, Deck's trail was picked up. He was chased through the Yorkshire Dales to his home base in Aysgarth, but couldn't stop because he'd been unable to lose his pursuers. He doubled back to the southwest and crossed the River Ribble. Still they came.

He pushed his horse on through the hilly forest and knew that he was getting dangerously close to Pendle Hill. That didn't bother him. In fact, it was his plan. He was counting on the widespread superstitious beliefs about the witches of Pendle Hill to cause the men who were after him to turn back.

It was a good plan, but they didn't turn back. They didn't even slow. Deck's horse was slowing and couldn't take much more. So when he saw a light in a cottage at the base of the hill, he galloped straight for it. There was a small barn off to the side that was visible by moonlight. He dismounted and pulled the horse in behind him.

Inside the cottage, Pleasant's mother asked if she'd heard something outside.

"I did," she said. "You stay inside. I'll go see."

Taking a lamp she went out into the night. It was cold and still. So she stopped and listened until she heard a horse's snuffle and stamp of the foot.

The barn door was closed even though she was sure she'd left it partially open. Inside she held up the lamp.

"Who's there?"

When Deck Durbin saw Pleasant illuminated by the lamp held aloft, he was so struck by her beauty that he temporarily forgot he was running for his life and, in fact, might have only minutes left to live.

"I, Beauty," he said stepping into the light so that she could see who had addressed her.

Pleasant was just as taken with the highwayman who had run into her barn to hide himself from authorities. She didn't particularly care what he'd done. What she cared about were the shiny chestnut curls that fell over his forehead and the warm golden-brown eyes that caused a flare of heat in deep in her heart and body.

"I'm running from the law," he said. "If they catch me they'll likely gibbet me."

"I see. Why did you think stopping here would help you? Don't you know where you are?"

"I do. But you don't look like a storybook witch." His eyes ran over her long, wavy black hair, pale green eyes, unnaturally red lips, and down to the nipples that stood erect from the cold pressing against the white underdress that showed above her black laced bodice.

"Appearances can be deceiving. Are you saying you're not afraid of me?"

He took a step closer wearing a smile that belied the danger he was in.

"Should I be?"

Before she had a chance to answer that question, he grabbed her and pulled her into a kiss. Pleasant was just under twenty, but had never been kissed. The fact that she was kissing a stranger in her barn was scandalous, but she didn't pull away. Her lips tingled from the contact that had ignited a fire.

When he pulled back, they both turned toward the sound of horses approaching.

Without thinking through all the implications and ramifications, Pleasant held both hands palm out in the direction of the sound and said something in a language Deck Durbin didn't know.

At once the sounds of shouting and hoof beats vanished.

"You're safe," she said.

He was reevaluating his position on fairytales. "What did you do?"

"I caused them to forget why they are out riding in the middle of the night."

He stared at her for a few beats before breaking into unrestrained laughter.

"Now what will you do for me?" she asked.

Deck came close, nuzzling her cheek, breathing on her neck, and said, "I have enough gold to go to Texas. Come with me. I'll make you my wife."

Pleasant Wimberley was a powerful witch who found herself powerless to access reason when she looked into the highwayman's eyes. She was also not of an age to weigh fully the consequences of impulsive decisions.

So she said, "Alright. I'll come with you, but make me your wife first."

"A Christian wedding?" He raised his eyebrows.

She laughed. "No. My mother will perform the rite. But make no mistake. You'll be bound nonetheless."

AND SO IT happened that they came to Texas in 1839, just a few years after the Battle of the Alamo. On the way to San Antonio, Pleasant pulled Deck to a stop.

She had a vision showing her that the road between San Antonio and Austin would become well-traveled. Pleasant recognized that the crossroads on the Blanco River and Cypress Creek would be an excellent site for an inn. That and, since she was pregnant by that time, the ride on the buckboard was very uncomfortable. She was ready to be done with the rigors of months of traveling.

Deck was dubious, but one look at the limestone ledges rising from the river was all he needed. They reminded him of home in Aysgarth and, taking that as a sign, he agreed to Pleasant's proposal.

Comanche raids were still common at the time, but warding the place against violence wasn't a particularly difficult task for Pleasant. For good measure, she extended the charm's range of effectiveness for twenty miles in every direction.

Deck was honest about his inclinations. He said he was no innkeeper, but he'd keep himself busy trading horses. His gift for spotting fast horses had kept him alive long enough to put together the gold necessary to strike out for Texas. There was no reason why he couldn't put it to good use.

FOR A YEAR they were happy. The Charmed Horse Inn had quickly gained a reputation as a place where travelers might get a good meal, a clean bed, and a good night's sleep. They had a little girl with her mother's black wavy hair and her father's golden eyes. Both parents doted on her like she was the first child ever born.

Deck was fairly certain he would never be apprehended so far from England, but thought it would be prudent for the family to take Pleasant's last name, which was Wimberley, just to be extra safe.

Try as he might, Deck couldn't remake himself into a family man. The dashing devil-may-care highwayman who exuded a sexy recklessness, had a heart that couldn't be tamed.

He left during the night and rode to San Antonio, attracted by the many tales he'd heard in the tavern. Tales of Spaniards, French, Creoles, civilized Indians, and half-breeds; all engaged in hunting buffalo or in contraband trade with Louisiana, which had been going on ever since Jean Lafitte had made Galveston a pirate base.

When Deck reached San Antonio and considered his options, he didn't fall in with buffalo hunters or contraband runners. He joined the Texas Rangers. It would have been ironic, highwayman turned lawman, except that it wasn't unusual for Rangers to have been on the other side of the law at some time or other.

When Pleasant realized Deck was gone, she was devastated and inconsolable. Not so much so that she was willing to turn the man she loved into a pig and serve him up in a bean and ham soup to customers at the tavern. But enough to raise the innate power of the crossroads, and use it in a spell to ensure that any witch who came to that locale would be courted only by a man besotted with true love.

What she didn't understand was that she *was* loved truly by Deck Durbin. It seems that love, even when potent and profound, cannot always prevail over a wild nature. When Deck got leave from the Rangers, or passed close to the Charmed Horse Inn, he would stay for a few days, make love to his wife, and kiss Pleasant's tears away in the night.

She lived from one visit to the next, but was occupied running a business and raising a family alone. Even though Deck visited a few times a year, he fathered two more daughters with Pleasant. All three were equally beautiful. And powerful.

The power of the spell she cast over the crossroads at Wimberley attracted witches from far and wide. Because after all, power centers act like magnets to witches.

In time the town that sprung up around the inn and horse ranch, would come to be called Wimberley after the witch who founded the settlement.

WIMBERLEY IS A magical place where local residents expect the unexpected.

Chapter One

So, yeah. Here I am in the Texas Hill Country wondering if I made the right call. I was given a travel allowance, but it didn't stretch far enough. I had to beg, borrow, scramble, and pawn to get enough money for a plane ticket from L.A. to Austin. But once I got on the plane, things started going my way.

Turned out I could get a limo from Austin to Wimberley for less than a one way bus ticket, taxi, or Uber. I have to laugh at that, but really I'm used to it. I may not get enough modeling/acting jobs to support a flea circus, but stuff like this happens to me. If I borrow a car, I get good parking places. If I need to supplement the rising star income with a bartender job, there's usually an opening at the exact place where I want to work.

Needless to say, I grabbed the limo opportunity with both hands and pulled up to downtown Wimberley in stretch-style. Black, of course. Naturally I was hoping somebody would tell the witches I arrived in style.

I'm one of the lucky ones holding a key to a single at the hotel. Single means double bed, but just one person. There are only sixteen rooms total and about a hundred guys, potential suitors like me, who were hoping to score a room at the Charmed Horse Hotel. I read the card in my room when I checked in.

Apparently there was a Charmed Horse Inn on this site almost two hundred years ago. The card said the place is famous for its location on the river and its ghost. Huh.

Somebody once told me that there are only two kinds of people, those who've seen ghosts and those who haven't. Those who report having a personal encounter believe in the supernatural. Those who haven't had a brush with unusual occurrences think it's primitive nonsense.

The guy who shared that wisdom at a bar many, many beers ago was wrong. I've never seen a ghost, but I'm not a hard ass skeptic either. I like to keep my opinion and belief options open until cornered.

I took the old-fashioned wide staircase down from my second story room that overlooked the river. When my foot hit the bottom step, I saw that there was a little crowd of about seven people standing around the woman who was playing a small town desk clerk.

Well, I guess it's not playing if desk clerk is her real life job. I usually just see things like that. All the world's a stage and all.

I stopped to listen. What can I say? I'm curious about attractions and these people are rapt.

"The original Charmed Horse Inn was just a few yards away. It was built in 1840 and torn down a hundred years ago. In the sixties, there was a tourist trap in this location. They sold, you know, local art, pralines, jackadillos, the usual Hill Country souvenirs. Lightning struck it one

Halloween night and burned it to the ground.

"What was built in its place was a café. It had a good run, popular with the locals, lasted about forty years. But right after the turn of the century, *this* century, workers just showed up one day, bulldozed the café and built the Wimberley Tavern. Five years later this hotel was built in the style of the Driskill in San Antonio. Smaller and not as luxurious, of course. So it looks old, like it was renovated, but it's not. It's new.

"Now as to the ghost. People say that at night, right outside, near the crossroads, if everything's quiet, sometimes you can hear galloping hoof beats. A few people say they've seen somebody dressed like a highwayman ride past and disappear. Others said they've seen a ghost in or around the tavern or here in the hotel dressed like a Texas Ranger.

"He wears a wide-brimmed hat, a loose-fittin' shirt, and a gun belt with holster and pistol. The old folks say it's Deck Wimberley, still looking out for his girls. Deck and his wife built the Charmed Horse Inn. She stayed, ran the inn and raised their girls, three of 'em, but he went rangerin'.

"Some say he's sorry he left his wife and can't move on until he thinks he's made up for it, but I don't know about that."

"Have you seen him?" a kid in a tee shirt and baseball cap asked.

The clerk shook her head. "I haven't seen him, but I've seen people right after they saw him. Those folks looked a fright. Made a believer out of me."

VICTORIA DANANN

JESUS. NO WONDER it's hard to get a room at this place. With a hook like that, this place is probably full year round.

I walked around the little group and headed out the front door.

Name is Willem, by the way. I know. Depending on who you talk to it's either pretentious or nostalgic. I guess, in my case, it was the second. My mom's great-great-grandfather on her mother's side was named Willem.

Circumventing the whole pretention/nostalgia speculation by calling myself Will is the easiest way to go. People assume it's short for William and that's okay with me. Not sure I understand why William is less pretentious than Willem, but whatever.

I grew up in Alabama, but headed for L.A. after two years at Alabama State. I took mostly core courses, but had a few classes in my chosen major, which was Metaphysics, Mythology, and Paranormal Psychology. I *loved* those classes. Gobbled up the info like a living vacuum and asked for more. The problem wasn't that I didn't want to study MMPP. The problem was that I didn't want to have to wade through Western Civ, English Composition, Algebra, Geology, a foreign language, and a host of other equally yawn-inspiring courses just to get to the good stuff.

The comments of all the people who'd told me that I was good-looking enough to be a movie star came back to me. I believed them. I mean, I have eyes and a mirror. Just sayin'. It sounded like a cool enough gig to me and I'd heard that there's a lot of time wasted on set when actors just sit around for hours. I have dark hair and eyes such a deep blue that people usually think they're black.

It's fun to watch the surprise when they see me in sunlight or bright lights and hear them go, "Hey. Your eyes are blue!" They always say it like they think I didn't know or that I've been deliberately hiding my eye color.

ANYWAY, IT SOUNDED like it could be the best of two worlds, earning mega-money while being able to study what I wanted to study independently, the old-fashioned way. Reading.

The first couple of cattle call auditions, I found out that my southern accent was going to be a problem.

I needed money for diction lessons, not to mention food, housing, clothing, etc. One of the guys waiting in line to audition told me that food and beverage service is the only way to go for wanna-be's because you can usually get a little schedule flexibility.

Tried waiting tables. That lasted all of two nights. So I located a bartending school. When I told the woman in the office I wasn't rolling in cake, but could pay a little at a time, she tilted her head to the side, smiled, and said, "That might not be a problem."

That's when I found out that "people" were right. My looks could open lesser doors on the way to stardom, if I was willing to get my body involved, enthusiastically.

You might say I went to bartending school on a fuck scholarship, which means I got a free ride, figuratively and literally, for getting off with a woman instead of my hand. I'm telling you. Life is strange.

Well, between my looks and my ability to do a few tricks, I did okay bartending, especially if I made liberal use of winks and *the* smile that made the one dimple pop out on the left side of my face. I had a no-drink rule for myself when I was working. If I was on the clock, I was all business. Afterward, I sometimes took advantage of the free drinks perk, the one the owner didn't need to know about. I guess technically that would be more a liberty than a perk, but whatever. I sat at the bar and had a drink or two when the cleanup crew was, well, cleaning up.

My days were regimented. Get up at noon. Call my agent. Yeah. I have an agent. Got her the same way I got through bartending school. I see if she has anything for me. If she doesn't, I show up at the new "spot" on Sunset Boulevard where people who have actual tip money come to experience "the scene". Even the dives have valet parking and secure lots for the beems, benzes, Porsches and Audis, along with the occasional Bentley or Lamborghini. They get to play like they're still relevant. I get tips. Everybody wins.

If she does have something, which – I gotta hand it to her – is more than half the time, I get copies of "Billboard" and "Variety" and go get in line with hundreds of other guys who migrated to L.A. because they were told they were pretty enough to be in movies and it sounded more exciting than whatever else they saw in their future.

I'm not dumb. I know it takes more than beauty. So I go to acting classes on Mondays and Wednesday. And let me tell you, they're not cheap. Every extra penny goes to coaches and diction lessons. The latter has caused my family to look at me like I have a rare and contagious disease.

"You sound like a Yankee, Will."

Believe me when I say that, in Alabama, that is *not* a compliment. Southerners take their southern accents seriously.

So, with the lessons, I can barely afford the half rent on the dump I share with a geek who's a Jabba the Hut look alike and never leaves the place. Hector gets enough freelance IT work to finance food and rent and the video game development he's sure will pay off big one day.

Can you imagine being named Hector and actually deciding to go by that? By kindergarten I would have shortened it to Heck or something not guaranteed to turn girls away.

Speaking of girls, it probably goes without saying that I never bring anybody home. Having a roommate like Hector is almost as much of a romance douser as being Hector.

Now you're caught up on my life. That's the last ten years in a nutshell. I got off the plane in L.A. when I was twenty and I'm celebrating thirty in another couple of months. Long story short, that means it's time to face facts. Make that fact in the singular because the only one that matters is this. If I was going to make it, it would have happened by now.

So reviewing my options. If I keep spinning wheels, maybe I'll wake up one day and find that another ten years is gone. Now I'm seeing forty looking back at me in the mirror, still living with Jabba, who leaves Taco Bell and

M&M wrappers everywhere. Or I could take control, make the "done" call, and head in another direction.

Told my sob story to the guy in line behind me and ended it with, "This is the last time I'm ever doing this. If this audition doesn't result in a paying job, I'm gone."

"You're quitting? Really?" he asked.

"Made up my mind. I'm a man, not a hamster."

"I hear that. So what are you gonna do?"

I smiled. "That's the question. Right?"

"Well, you're cute for sure. And straight, right?" I drew back as far as I could without getting out of line. "No, man, I'm not trying to get in your pants. I'm just saying," he leaned in closer and lowered his voice to a whisper, "that, if you're straight, you're cute and buff enough to try for the witches."

I gave him my best what-the-fuck look, thinking I was in line in front of somebody who'd snapped from one too many mass auditions, but I decided to go with it. Who knows why?

"What witches?"

"You know."

I shook my head. "No. I don't know."

After a few beats he laughed, right in my face. "How could you have *never* heard about the," he looked around, "you know?"

"Maybe I keep to myself. Look. I don't want to be rude, but you're edging toward annoying. If you've got something to say, spit it out."

He slipped his backpack down his arm and let it drop to the ground. He rifled through it and came up with a card. "Here it is. It's not doing me any good because, you know, I like boys. So you might as well have it. Maybe it'll do you some good. If you're really quitting."

"I'm really quitting," I said, as I looked down at the card in his hand. I don't know what made me reach out and take it. Maybe curiosity. Maybe the fact that my life had been almost as predictable as a hamster wheel for nearly ten years.

Wake up.

Call agent.

If there's a morning audition, shower and find a way there. If there's an afternoon audition, go back to bed until noon, then shower and find a way there.

Eat at the deli counter.

Report for bar duty at eight.

Work until two.

Have a drink on the house.

Here you can insert random girl hookup. I say random because I'm not interested in anyone in particular, but there's no such thing as a night when some lush babe isn't interested in extracurriculars with moi. I'm not in the mood every night because I'm not fourteen. At least that's what I tell myself, maybe I'm bored with the chicks, too.

Go to the pad shared with dweeb.

Sleep.

Wake up.

Well, you get it.

I FIGURED I could use an adventure. Alright, well, calling a phone number on a card might not sound like much of an adventure, but he did say witches were involved. So that sounded like fertile ground for possibilities. Right?

YOU PROBABLY KNOW what happened next.

That's right. Not only did I not get a job out of the audition, I never had a chance to speak one word. They just took one look at me and said, "Wrong." Then waved me off like they were the mad King George.

Did I say I'd be done? Well, I'm a man of my word.

Usually.

So done. Done. Done.

Got an Uber home and he probably gave me a bad review because I really did not feel chatty. Usually I sit in the front seat and try to make the day a little less long for people trying to eke out a subsistence living. Especially since I know that for a lot of them, it's a second job and the mileage is steadily ticking toward the reaper. That means the inevitable day when that vehicle is going to need tires and / or repairs that outdistance driver proceeds.

Come to think of it, I'm done with this city, too. I mean, who knows? Maybe the worst thing that could have happened to me was making it. I don't want to be the guy who buys five-thousand-dollar pants and quibbles over whether I'm going to make eighty million or eighty one million for a month's work. Jesus.

So Uber man, who really was a nice enough sort, pulled over to the curb of my shitty built-in-the-fifties-and-not-well-maintained apartment building. I saw him lean out and look. While he was doing his dashboard computer thing, I tried to see it through his eyes.

Sure. I could say something like, "It's not a nice address, but it's a funky address, goddamn it," but who would I be kidding. It's shit. That's what I've made of the last ten years, the potentially most productive, conclusively most marketable years of my entire life. Shit.

I closed the door. Hector looked up from his work station, which was spread across most of what had once been a living room, and nodded vaguely. I waved half-heartedly, headed for the privacy of my room, closed the door, dropped the backpack on the bed and sat down beside it.

It didn't take long to fish out the card. Once I had it in my hand, I sat there on the side of the bed studying the text, graphics, colors, even the textures. It was a heavy-weight vellum that felt almost like fabric, cotton maybe. When I rubbed my finger over it, I realized the text was raised like old-style engraving. All things combined to make it not just draw attention, but compel.

Maybe the designer was a psychologist, but I really felt like I had to reach in my pocket, pull out my phone, and dial the number. There wasn't even a hint as to what I'd be calling about.

Maybe it was a retirement home for psuedo actors who never even got called back for a cop/doctor/lawyer show walk-on.

What would I say if they answered? *"Hey. I have no idea why I'm calling. Some random dude standing in a moo chute audition line gave me this card and said that if I was really moving on from acting to check out the, um, witch-*

es?"

It sounded lame when I played it over in my mind. If I was on the receiving end of that call, I'm fairly certain I would hang up on me.

The hum of the little fridge in my room drew my attention. I often thought of it as my own personal version of a Hummer. So I got up and pulled a cold diet drink out. When I closed the fridge door, the hum quietened, which was unusual to the point of being rare. When I opened the can, the crack of aluminum sounded loud, like I was in an echo chamber. I supposed that's what the space would sound like all the time without Hummer noise.

Sitting back down on the side of my unmade bed, I took a long pull on the aspartame poison, chasing the Scotch neat I'd borrowed for a nightcap at The Spot, and held the card up again. After studying it for a few more minutes, it became clear that it wasn't going to give up any more information than before. So I put it on the bedside stand next to my trusty alarm and the bendy-neck lamp, dropped my clothes on the floor, climbed in bed, and turned off the light.

I lay awake for a few minutes thinking how strange it was to know the alarm wouldn't be going off in the morning. I wondered if Julie would realize I hadn't called. Seemed to me that I should feel something about pushing through the exit-only door. Since I'd dedicated a decade of my young life to the single-minded focus of becoming the next Brad Pitt, you would think I'd be depressed or morose or angry. But honestly, I didn't feel any of those things.

The fact that I had no Plan B wasn't scaring me or worrying me either. And that worried me. I should be worried. Right? That's what a normal person would feel in my situation.

Telling myself that I'd delve into the metaphysical mysteries of personal self-reflection after a good night's sleep, I turned over and shut my eyes.

Keep in mind that I used the phrase "good night's sleep". If that was a qualifier, then the night was disqualified. Whenever I dozed off, I found myself dreaming about every Hollywood version of witch-type characters I'd ever seen, from the high school girls in *The Craft* to the harpies subbing for Dracula's vampire wives in *Van Helsing*.

Waking myself each time I was a hair's breadth away from being groped, clawed, bitten or seduced, my eyes were drawn to the card pretending to sit innocently on my bedside table. I'm not going to say it glowed in the dark, but I will say that I knew where it was. After several hours of tossing and turning, I threw back the covers, grabbed the card in sleepy disgust, and put it inside the Hummer.

"There," I said, throwing myself back onto the bed.

Twenty minutes later I imposed lucid dreaming on a dream wherein a succubus was about to suck up a lot more than my dick. She was going for the full monty, body and soul.

I jackknifed up, which put me in a sitting position looking straight at the Hummer that was vibrating away three feet from the end of my bed.

"Christ," I said to no one.

My eyes wandered all around the fridge. I'd built

makeshift bookcases with cinder blocks and boards from Home Depot and, in ten years, I'd collected an impressive library. Mostly from the half-price store. It's amazing what treasures people are willing to give away or sell for pennies on the dollar.

Anyway, I thought about fishing out one of the tomes that really is a lullaby in printed word form, but I knew if I turned on the light I wouldn't go back to sleep.

In a huff, I threw myself onto my right side and forced my mind to think about a jumping sheep. Not just any sheep. I'd seen a video featuring a sheep who'd been orphaned young and taken in by an Aussie family with Border Collies. The poor sheep thought she was a Border Collie and tried to play with the dogs, who were not the least species-confused. They just stared with a dog version of a WTF expression. I felt sorry for the shunned sheep who so desperately wanted to be accepted.

That's what was on my mind when I drifted off the last time.

The next time I woke there were cracks of light around my thick-lined dark curtains. That didn't mean I got a full night's sleep. There were usually only two to three hours of darkness left when I turned in at night.

Life and times of a barkeep.

Turning toward the alarm, I opened one eye so I could read the time. Nine-oh-seven. The first thought that jumped to mind after that was that it probably wasn't too early to call the number on *the card.*

Half falling out of bed, half pulling myself up, I headed to the shared bath outside my door. Jabba's door was closed and I didn't hear any signs of life. It was a tiny slice of heavenly experience, the times when I could pretend that I was actually alone.

Having relieved myself of the burden of Scotch, diet drinks, and vitamin waters, I stepped back into my room and looked at the Hummer. I had the oddest compulsion to take a shower and shave before making that call. I'd figured out by the time I was ten that feelings like that usually mean something and had started paying attention to them.

You might call it intuition. You might call it weirdness, but calling something weird doesn't make it go away. It also doesn't make it untrue.

I guess that's what drew me to study MMPP. I find that, if you keep your eyes open and don't shut down possibilities before they have a chance to show themselves, you'll find that life is far stranger than most people are ready to admit. By the time I was twelve I was calling this vague and invisible sense of guidance the Voice. Not that it had an actual voice. And not that I called it that anywhere except inside my own head. Even as a child I was savvy enough to figure out that telling other people about voices could land you in the Counselor's office when everybody else was outside for recess.

That was the long meandering way of explaining why I went back to the bathroom, used the good soap, gave myself a twenty-dollar shave and used just enough product on my hair to give myself the almost-impossible-to-pull-off-bedhead-by-design look. Over torn jeans I buttoned up a clean, pressed button down, left the shirt tail out and put a good-looking Armani sweater on over. The fashionable juxtaposition of rags and riches was hip and looked good if I did say so myself.

Too much trouble for a guy who's straight, you say? I'd agree with you completely, but the gay boys taught me that women like clothes and don't appreciate the practice of looking like you reached into the closet wearing a blindfold and put on whatever your hand came back with. If you want to be noticed by powerful women who can do something for you, you need to dress in a way that comes off as understated sexy. I've worked at that look and pretty much mastered it, even if I do say so myself.

After transforming into cover model perfection, I took a look at the room and decided that the bed should be made before the phone call. Don't ask me why. I know it doesn't make sense. I know it sounds squirrelly. After all, I wasn't planning a video call, but the Voice was insistent. So I took three minutes to make the bed. I even picked clothes up off the floor and put them in the duffel that I lugged to the laundry downstairs when it couldn't possibly wait another day.

With an environment that was semi-presentable and a personal presentation that would cause most women's mouths to water, I was ready. Or I would be after coffee.

I was more scared of venturing into the kitchen than I was of my lack of a plan for the future, but like the macho southern man I was, I forged ahead.

There was no window in the kitchen, but there was a slider door and balcony on the other side of the dinette. I flipped on the light and, more or less, stood there frozen. I may have gaped. I'm not sure. I know I was surprised.

The kitchen was spotless. Everything was in its place, whether drawer, cupboard, or cabinet and the surfaces almost gleamed. I must tell you that I'd *never* seen the kitchen like that in all the years I'd call that dump home. I realized for the first time that I hadn't known what the kitchen looked like. Not really.

As if that wasn't spooky enough, the coffee machine had been set up with water and coffee in a fresh filter. We had an old-style setup, but I promised myself that some-day I would have one of those single cup doobies. Fancy. For sure.

Hell. Maybe Hector was turning over a new leaf, too. If he was, I'd have to stop thinking of him as Jabba. I mean a kitchen *that* clean deserves some respect. Coffee ready-to-go deserves respect plus long-lasting friendship.

So I turned the machine on and leaned against the counter smiling.

On the very day I should have been drowning my sor-rows in country music and alcohol, dreading taking a bus to sweet home Alabama, and dragging my ass into my parents' house to say, "Surprise! I'm a thirty-year-old without a degree. My only viable skill is that I can tend bar and I'm living with you again."

That should have made me depressed enough to think about taking a carousel ride on the Santa Monica Pier and then jumping off. Of course, that probably wouldn't be a solution because I'm a really strong swimmer. Survival instinct would kick in and force me to swim to shore. The idea of not being able to commit suicide by drowning was depressing. Or it should be. But I *didn't* feel depressed. At all.

The only part of that scenario that was appealing was the carousel ride. Now that I think about it, I might be a little depressed about that last part because, after all, I am a grown man and, as such, know that it's out of sorts with my image to find merry-go-rounds fascinating.

That was the stream of consciousness that was lazily filtering through my head while I waited for the coffee pot to do that gurgling hissing thing it does right at the end of the cycle to indicate it's finished. Or dying.

I stirred sugar and coffee cream into the cup and then stood there wondering what to do with the spoon. A kitchen that looked showroom pristine just shouldn't be spoiled with an errant spoon. So I rinsed it off. Thoroughly. Dried it. And put it back in the drawer.

No one the wiser.

It had been the most in-depth and complicated preparation for a phone call in the history of Alexander Graham Bell. All was done. No more delays or excuses.

So I returned to my room, closed the door and, for reasons I wouldn't be able to explain, locked it. I retrieved the card from the Hummer and set it on the bedspread next to the phone. What a fine pair of items they made. A phone and its reason for existing, a potential call.

Taking a deep breath like I was embarking on breaking a channel-swim record, I dialed the number on the card. Now I was holding the phone next to my ear with one hand and holding the card with the other so that I could continue looking at it while I waited for an answer. I sat the card down and took a sip of coffee.

Ringing stopped. "Mr. Draiocht." This was said by a man with an English accent and a no-nonsense business-like tone.

I sat blinking trying to assess how I felt about the witches knowing my name.

"How did you know my name?"

I heard a distinct sigh on the other end of the connection before the man said, "Caller ID."

"Oh. Of course."

"What can I do for you, Mr. Draiocht?"

"I don't know. I was given your card. And I guess I thought that was the question I'd be asking you. What can you do for me?"

"Ah. I see. What do you know about our program?"

"Nothing."

There was a slight, but distinct pause. "If you'd like to attend the next Orientation, you may be admitted if you pass an evaluation to be conducted at the door."

"What kind of evaluation?"

"Nothing for which you can prepare. You are either right for the program or you are not."

"Oh. When's the next Orientation?"

"This evening. A car will pick you up at six thirty if you want to move forward."

Part of me was thinking that bad things begin with mysteries, but I checked in with the Voice and it was quiet. While the Voice might allow me to do stupid shit or unproductive shit, the Voice intervened if I was about to do something irrevocably dumb or dangerous.

"Okay," I said. "My address…"

"We can find it. Don't be late. Dinner will be included."

"Uh, wait! What do I wear?"

"What you have on is fine."

"How do you know what I'm wearing?"

"I don't know what you are or aren't wearing, but approval does not depend upon clothes. You are either right for the program or you are not."

He didn't wait for a reply. The next thing I heard was a series of three beeps letting me know the call had been disconnected.

"Okay. Bye. See you later," I said to the room with sarcasm.

I know what you're thinking. You're thinking that a sane man, one who's been to the movies at some point in his life, would not even consider going, Voice or no Voice. You're right, of course. That's what a sane man would do.

It would be an exaggeration to say that I had nothing to lose at that point because it was far from true. I had my books. And my life. But it would be fair to reiterate that I was a man without a plan. I wasn't desperate, but I was curious and certain that, if I didn't show up at the curb at six-thirty, I'd spend the rest of my life wondering what would have happened at Orientation.

Time to walk the walk. What student of the paranormal would refuse the opportunity to attend an Orientation possibly leading to some sort of "program" involving witches.

Again, I know what you're thinking and, again, no,

I'm not ignorant enough to believe we're talking about cartoon witches like Disney or supernatural hags like those in Macbeth. I assumed these "witches" were modern-day Wiccans, a sect of pagans with little, if any, verifiable power to affect reality.

It seemed I was all cleaned up with no place to go at the moment, but I did need to call and cancel my shift at The Stop. The bar manager was not happy because it was Friday. Lots of upper, upper middle class people liked to celebrate surviving another work week with the corporate version of the MAN by alcohol-induced letting loose. Friday nights were good for the bar and good for me.

"You don't show tonight, Will, don't come back."

That's what he said to me. My mind raced around. Was I willing to cut the only tie between me and script from the U.S. Treasury? I must be a gambler because I didn't really hesitate.

"Okay. I'll be in to get the rest of my tips Monday afternoon."

Wolfie, the bar manager, huffed and disconnected.

Had people forgotten how to say goodbye?

As I looked around my room, my eyes landed on the clock. I had eight hours to fill until go-time. For the second time that day I found myself smiling, just because of the simple pleasure of recreation time. I couldn't remember the last time I'd had a whole day to read.

I settled on a book from the Duke Parapsychology Lab that I'd acquired weeks before and hadn't had time to dive into. I kicked off my boots, bounced on the bed, and said to hell with perfect bedhead. A couple of hours later my stomach rumbled loud enough to be heard over the Hummer and reminded me that coffee had been breakfast. It was good, but it doesn't stay with you.

So I slipped into sloppy deck shoes, grabbed the book, and walked down to the corner Chinese. The place was filled with the overriding and heavenly aroma of eggrolls becoming little golden, hot grease masterpieces. Of all other cultures, Chinese come closest to Southerners in understanding that deep fried equals nirvana. I ordered a special with a diet drink, sat down at a vinyl covered dinette table in the corner and proceeded to enjoy my day off. If days off were about to become a lot more common than was comfortable, I would think about that some other time.

When I returned to the apartment, Hector was working at his station, which also seemed to have had a Martha Stuart makeover. Neat. Clean. Everything put away. Not even any wrappers in the trash can. I noticed that the overhaul had generalized to his personal presentation as well. He appeared to be wearing clean clothes, but the most shocking thing was how Hector looked with trimmed beard and clean combed hair. I'm not sure I would have recognized him on the street.

"Hey," I said.

"Hey," he responded.

"What's going on?"

"What do you mean?"

"Well, the place is kind of presentable. As are you. Something you want to tell me about?"

He shrugged. "You can't have order of thought in

chaos."

"A sound philosophy. Well, it's an improvement. Nobody'll argue with that."

"What are you doing here?"

"I live here."

"Not really."

"I have somethin' special tonight and I quit acting."

"You quit acting? Does that mean you got an acting job and quit?"

"Don't be mean. I've officially decided that acting is not for me and I'm moving on."

"Huh. Does that mean you're also moving out?"

"Got no plans as of yet, but you'll be the first to know."

"I will need fair notice."

"Yeah. Goes without sayin'."

Hector turned back to his monitor. Chitchat was over.

Closed my door, lay down with my book, which was enthralling, but not so enthralling that it could overcome the bio-dip that occurs after a nice greasy lunch. So I fell asleep.

When I woke I rolled over and looked at the clock. Six-fifteen.

I jackknifed off the bed like I had a trampoline for a mattress and ran for the bathroom. Thank God I didn't have any pillow wrinkles on my face. My right side was a little pink-looking but that would settle on the ride to wherever.

I threw water in my eyes and spritzed my hair where it had been squashed and looked like actual bedhead. The shirt might be a little mussed but didn't scream, "I took a nap in these clothes." So I jumped back into the boots, grabbed the coolest pair of shades I own, the Wayfarers, and made it to the curb at six twenty-nine.

CHAPTER TWO

F OR ALMOST A minute I contemplated that the whole thing might be some sort of prank. Here I was standing on a curb waiting for a car without a clue what to look for, driven by a stranger, to an unidentified place for an unidentified purpose, all while being videoed for future TV airing and humiliation. My voluntary participation in this madness was sounding crazy even to myself.

My head turned to the left just as the Bentley turned the corner my way. It wasn't just me. Every other head on the street turned to look at the car. It was a thing of beauty, a deeply polished bronze color with chrome trim. It pulled to a stop in front of me and the driver got out. She was a cute, perky redhead with natural carrot-colored hair partially covered by a chauffeur's cap. The rest of her uniform consisted of a white tank top, black jacket, black leggings and black ballet slippers.

She bounced around to my side of the car with a megawatt smile. "Mr. Draiocht, I presume?"

I smiled. "Call me Will."

"Against the rules, Mr. Draiocht," she said as she opened the door to the back seat. "I'm Chatsworth."

"Good name for a chauffeur."

As Chatsworth closed the door and went around the car, my fingers ran over the mocha-colored leather. Let me just say that I'd never been able to shop in a store that sold jackets made with that quality of leather. It was buttery smooth, supple to the touch and I was thinking that I would have no trouble giving up acting and bartending for a life that included rides like that.

When she pulled away, I said, "Where are we headed?"

"Malibu."

"Malibu! On a Friday night? I hope you have snacks and a full tank because that's going to take hours."

She giggled. "We'll see. I have some waters and wine coolers on ice. Are you hungry now?"

"No. I'm fine."

"Please let me know if you change your mind. Would you like to listen to music? Eagles maybe?"

I watched her glance at me in the rearview mirror. What kind of spooky guess was that? Nobody my age listened to Eagles. But it just so happened that I did. They formed a bridge between the country my family listened to and the pop most women gravitated to.

"How did you know I like The Eagles?"

She smiled. "Hey. It's a beautiful California evening. What could be more perfect for a drive from Hollywood out to Malibu?"

Well, she had me there. Nothing could possibly be more perfect than that. "Yes. I would love to listen to Eagles on the way. So, how long have you been driving for this, um, outfit?"

"I'm sorry, Mr. Draiocht. I'm not allowed to talk about

myself. I will, however, listen if you would like to talk about you."

I laughed. "Eagles it is," I said.

I would have expected the usual stop-and-go gridlock because we were on the road at the busiest traffic moment of the week, and you've seen the L.A. freeways in the movies and on TV, right? But we sped through town, hit all the lights and turned onto Pacific Coast Highway One at Santa Monica. It was nice gliding along next to the water, listening to The Eagles. It was so nice that, when we pulled through a gate onto the circular drive of a house tucked back in the Malibu Hills, I couldn't have begun to tell you how we got there. Either I'd been lost in thought or enchanted by music.

The most miraculous thing was that it was not yet seven thirty when the car pulled up to the grand entrance of a structure that looked more like a palace than a home. It was impossible that the drive could have been made in that time. And yet it had.

"Here we are," she said as the engine went silent.

I waited for her to come around to my door. If she wanted to play the role to the hilt, I wasn't going to be a barrier to performance. She opened my door and, as I was getting out of the car, one of the two massive doors opened. A guy who looked way too much like Lurch from the Addams Family came out and stood on the landing, apparently waiting for me. The fact that the entrance was up six steps made him appear even taller than his sock-feet seven foot height.

I turned to the little redhead. "It was a pleasure,

Chatsworth."

"Likewise, Mr. Draiocht," she smiled. "I'm sure you'll be admitted to the Orientation, but I'll wait just in case."

I took that as reassurance that I was not about to be dinner, although the lyrics of "Hotel California" were suddenly at the forefront of my mind.

Sensing my reticence, Lurch gestured toward the entry and said, "This way Mr. Draiocht."

I went ahead and stopped a few feet inside, awaiting instructions. The foyer was every bit as palatial as I'd suspected, given the price-per-square-inch of the property the house was sitting upon. I didn't have time to take everything in before Lurch said, "Please wait in here."

He'd shown me into a small comfortable-looking office behind French doors to the right. Nothing sinister-looking. I stepped in, took a seat in front of the desk, and waited, but not for long.

In less than a minute a sleek-looking, raven-haired beauty click-clacked in on thin high heels, wearing a black figure-hugging suit and a white silk blouse. She even wore her hair pulled back into a bun, the slight concession to modernity being that it was more or less messy. The outfit would have met the corporate manual for women using battering rams against the glass ceiling if not for the smoky eyes and the siren-red lipstick.

I'm sure she saw me take her in head to toe even though I made half an effort to do it surreptitiously. I would definitely do her. I was imagining pulling out that spike holding her hair in place and loosening that tight-fitted jacket. The chest she was hiding was very promising and clearly in need of being freed from restrictive clothing.

That fantasy dissolved when she said, "Mr. Draiocht?"

I jerked my gaze from her chest to her eyes and said, "Yes. That's me."

She smiled, sat down, took the paperclip off the stack of pages she'd brought with her and began leafing through them. She glanced at me a couple of times as she was scanning, eyes moving fast, but kept her eyes to the paper when she asked her first question.

"I see you've been seeking work as an actor."

I cleared my throat and sat up a little straighter. "That's right. Seeking being the operative word."

"No luck?" Keeping her head down in reading position, she looked up at me from under her eyelashes.

I gave her my best smile, hoping to look like I didn't care. "No," I shook my head.

She nodded. "If you're not admitted to Orientation tonight, what's your plan?"

The guy on the phone told me I couldn't prepare, and I wasn't prepared for that question. So I stalled.

"I didn't get your name?"

She gave me a smile that broadcast that I'd been caught stalling. "Ms. Blackwell."

"I've been moving in one direction for ten years and only decided yesterday that I'm done. I haven't really had time to contemplate what's next."

"I like honest answers. Actors have a tendency to improvise on the spot. It's always easiest on everybody to just tell the truth."

"Well, I'm glad you feel that way because, *honestly*, I

don't know why I'm here."

She graced me with the same brilliant smile I'd been given when she entered. I'd call it the first-impression smile. "I'm sure you think that's unusual, but it's far more common than not. We don't recruit, you see. We simply let the right people find us."

I nodded as if I'd just absorbed something profound, even though I knew nothing more than I had prior to stating that I didn't know why I was there.

"Would you like something to drink while we're finishing up?"

"No. Thank you. I'm fine."

"Very well. I see here that you're from Alabama, but your speech doesn't give any hint of that."

I shrugged. "I've spent the last ten years and a truck-load of money working on getting rid of any hint of that."

"Well, it worked. If I wasn't reading your file, I would have guessed Illinois."

"Yeah, well, speaking of that file…"

"You've made it as far as the foyer office, Mr. Draiocht. Trust me, that's a little bit of an accomplishment all in itself. It's not a guarantee of admission to the Orientation, but only a handful of young men in the area get this far."

My lips parted, ready to give voice to the appropriate response, whenever it came to mind. Unfortunately that response never gelled in my head. She went on.

"What do you like to do with your free time?"

That was easy and the answer wasn't especially in-criminating so I didn't hesitate. "Read."

"Hmmm. What do you like to read?"

"Non-fiction."

She set the papers down and focused a laser-intensive look on my face that made me want to squirm in my chair.

"Are you being evasive?"

"Not at all. Most people are either not really interested in what I read or don't know what it is when I tell them."

Her smile and affable manner was gone. She was all business. "I'm not *most* people, Mr. Draiocht."

Of course I'd already known that, but the way she said '*most* people' made it sound like that was the worst thing someone could be.

"No offense intended. I read books about mythology and all kinds of metaphysical theory. Sometimes paranormal research catches my eye."

Her assessing manner remained firm, but a small smile reappeared. "So you're still interested in the subjects you studied in school."

"Yes."

"If you had no worries, unlimited resources, and lots of free time, is that what you would do with your life? Read?"

"Unlimited resources and lots of free time?"

"Yes."

"It sounds like one of those 'what if a genie offered you three wishes' questions. I've never indulged in *that* kind of fantasy before."

"You strike me as the sort who can process quickly."

It was clear she was waiting for an answer and just as clear that, if I wanted to move on in the process, I needed to give one.

"Yes. I would like to delve into things I've never had time to study."

"See. That wasn't so hard."

"Maybe not for someone who hasn't read a lot about wish-givers and how much trouble the wish-maker can make for themselves by giving the wrong answer."

She laughed out loud. "I'm not a genie and it wasn't a trick question."

"If you say so."

She nodded and sat back, studying me as if she could penetrate my mind and read my thoughts if she concentrated hard enough.

"Very well, Mr. Draiocht. I'm going to pass you on to Orientation. There will be a brief video presentation during dinner." When she stood, I stood. She walked around the desk and extended her hand. I took it. "Congratulations," she said. "You're in. And best of luck."

"Thank you."

With no idea what I was thanking her for, I decided that video and dinner sounded okay so, at that point, there was no reason to not see the thing through.

Following my inquisitor out the door I was again intercepted by Lurch. "This way, Mr. Draiocht."

At that point I'd been addressed formally so many times that I was beginning to think I might get used to being called Mr. Draiocht.

He led me down the grand hallway, which was twelve feet wide and lined with art that looked both medieval and expensive. Lots of depictions of banquets and bacchanalia.

The collector was clearly fond of food and wine. Possibly sex as well.

Stopping before another set of French doors, Lurch turned to me and gestured toward a room with no windows, but lots of ambiance including gas-lit wall sconces. "This way, Mr. Draiocht. Sit anywhere you like. Anywhere that's available, that is."

Nodding toward him, I took in the room. The ceiling was coffered. The walls were lined with polished blocked rosewood. The wood floor was wide distressed planks mostly hidden by a luxuriously thick and intricately designed carpet in tones of sage and red, more Venetian than Oriental. The art featured curling branches with delicate leaves and would have been worth a longer look if not for the fact that I was taking in the rest of the setup.

The table was arranged in a u-shape and set for five people with the most elegant linen, table, and glassware I'd ever seen. My mother would have gone nuts. No doubt about it. I was tempted to take out my phone, grab a photo and send it to her, but concluded that behavior might disqualify me for whatever I was competing for. If that statement sounds ridiculous to you, it's not just you. I think it's ridiculous, too. It's also the real reason why I didn't do it; because she would ask me where I was and what I was doing. Then what would I say?

I might also have to explain the four other guys standing around holding crystal brandy or whiskey tumblers, looking sexy and elegant enough for a Ralph Lauren ad. A little roughing up and anyone of them would be hired by Guess or Abercrombie in a heartbeat.

Yes. I noticed they had cover-model looks. When guys say they don't evaluate the way other guys look, they're lying pure and simple. Knowing somebody is pretty doesn't mean you want to fuck 'em.

So my eyes scanned the guys who seemed to be chatting amiably in a loose huddle. Their posture was a study in relaxed posing, the old one-hand-in-pocket sort of thing. They returned the favor and gave me a thorough look-over. I wouldn't say I read forthright hostility on their faces, but they didn't seem eager to welcome the new kid in town.

Movement caught my eye and I turned in time to see the back wall open where I hadn't noticed there was a door before. Someone dressed like a waiter came toward me with a smile. "Would you care for an aperitif, Mr. Draiocht?"

"Sure," I said. "What ya' got?"

He smiled at my deliberately casual answer. "Let's just say it would be hard for you to name something we don't have."

I laughed at that. I wasn't a bartender for nothing. "A Commonwealth?"

The waiter raised an eyebrow but smiled in a self-satisfied way. "No problem."

"No problem?" I asked with a good dose of incredulity. "How about a Rum Martinez?"

He didn't hesitate. "Your choice," he said, "although I would recommend the Commonwealth before dinner and the Rum Martinez after."

"Hmm. What's your name?"

The man looked like no one had ever asked and for a moment I thought he'd been struck dumb. He looked as if he was debating whether or not to give it. "Bartolo, sir."

"*Bar*tolo?" I laughed. "A perfect name for a master of the bar." He grinned. "Well, Bartolo, your advice is well-received. I will try your Commonwealth before dinner and look forward to a Rum Martinez after."

"Very good, Mr. Draiocht." With a small nod, he disappeared behind a chunk of blocked paneling that, apparently, swung in and out seamlessly. Nice.

I walked over to the four other diners, who had stopped talking to each other. "So do you think the room has audio or video surveillance or both?" I asked the group at large.

The four of them immediately began looking around nervously, searching for signs of technology, as if it hadn't occurred to them that they were being observed. And maybe it hadn't.

"Just kidding," I said. "Name's Will."

The guy nearest me stuck out his hand and I shook it. "I'm Harper," he said. "You really think they've been recording everything we've said?" He had the look of a blue blood descendant who'd been raised on a Malibu surfboard without a care in the world. He was tan, with blond highlights that didn't look salon-generated, and hair that was unapologetically over-the-collar. He was wearing a soft mauve crew neck tee over slacks with a lightweight sports coat. If he showed up at my bar looking like that, he'd have fifty women wanting to pay good money for a night.

I smiled and shrugged before letting my eyes move on. Robert looked like he'd spent the day on the top floor of a Fortune 500 company. Expensive suit, raw silk tie, definitely no hair touching his collar. His hair barely dared to touch his head.

Charlie was handsome, but he was also a mean-looking son-of-a-gun, whose persona was completely out of step with his fashion sense. He wore pleated khaki pants with crisp ironed seams, a pink button-down with a maroon tie, and flip flops.

Last was Ivan. Ivan was tall, lean, tan, and had a smile kissed by bleach. He wore newish-looking jeans under a coat and tie. On impulse I asked, "What do you do for a living, Ivan?"

"Tennis pro. Bellaire."

"Sweet," I said.

I couldn't imagine how this guy thought life was going to treat him better than that, but I supposed he had his reasons for being there just like the rest of us.

"How about you?" he asked.

"Bartender."

"Oh." He smiled. "So that's what that was about with the drinks."

"Yeah," I said. "Thought I might as well have some fun with this. Although I don't really know what *this* is." I chuckled, but as I did I saw the others exchange glances. "Oh. So I'm the only one? You all know what you're doing here."

Harper opened his mouth to say something, but I'll never know what it was going to be because Bartolo whisked in.

"Please take your seats, gentlemen. Dinner is about to be served."

Robert and Charlie headed straight for the chairs on the end. Harper and Ivan took seats next to them. That left me in the middle, at the top of the horseshoe curve, furthest from the screen. But it's not like I cared. I mean it wasn't like musical chairs where the last person doesn't get a seat at the table.

As soon as I, the last to sit down, had taken my chair, the room came alive with wait staff. One person was pouring wine while another set an assorted basket of freshly baked breads while another set out individual saucers of butter pads stamped with the crest that was on the gates, the front doors, and in the grand foyer.

I turned to Ivan and said, "Top drawer. Bet they can't beat this in Bellaire."

He smirked like it was just any other day, but said, "Yeah. A guy could get used to this."

The waiters delivering food drew my attention. It appeared that each of the five of us had his own personal waiter. It also seemed that each of us was getting a different first course.

Robert got Caesar salad. Harper got oysters on the half shell. Charlie got onion soup. Ivan got what appeared to be caramelized mushrooms on watercress. I got coconut shrimp. My favorite.

I turned to Harper. "Is that your favorite?"

"It is. Kind of scary how much they know about us, but in a way it's relaxing. They already know the good, the bad, and the ugly. And we're still here."

"I can see how that could take the pressure off." I was getting the distinct impression that I was the *only* one who didn't know the entire story on why we were here. So I decided to enjoy dinner, watch the presentation and see if I could piece the puzzle together later. I would have felt like a fraud except that I was an actor by profession, which meant that I flitted from one dishonest vignette to another.

The lights dimmed simultaneously as strains of acoustic guitar flowed from what was arguably the best sound system I'd ever heard. I would have sworn they were hiding the actual guitarist behind the wall. Two large squares of block paneling slid to the side with a low whirring noise that was barely noticeable, to expose a giant black glass screen.

The room was just dark enough to make video look good and just light enough to be able to see and appreciate the beauty of dinner. I hadn't had food like that since I was being courted by my agent.

I popped a jumbo coconut shrimp in my mouth and grabbed the dark roll sitting atop my personal bread basket. As a believer in 'signs', I figured the dark roll wanted to be consumed first.

The acoustic guitar faded out and was replaced by sounds of nature as the first image appeared. It was a giant of a man who looked like a fantasy movie Viking, long blonde hair partly braided around his face, with beard scruff that was more red than blonde. He was wearing faded jeans, a black Henley that showed off part of his prominent clavicle, sleeves pushed up to show off muscular forearms, and black biker boots.

He was different from the guys in the room with me, but no less attractive in his own way. Just depends on whether or not giant guys with blonde hair, blue eyes, square jaws, and hard-looking-stomachs do it for you. He was standing in front of an emerald green river with limestone ledges in the background and cypress trees with exposed roots in the foreground.

"Hey," he said, "I'm Raider."

Raider? I didn't find that at all difficult to believe.

"Right now you're probably thinking this looks too magical to be real," he said with a twinkle in his eye, "but this isn't even the river's best day. I've seen the water change from emerald green to turquoise on a sunny day and go black as night in a thunder storm. It's not magic though. It's Wimberley."

He began walking slowly along the grassy bank of the river as he talked. "The first Wimberley came here before Texas was even a republic and the family's been here ever since. Some of us are married to the descendants. Some of us are married to newcomers." He laughed. "Of course, newcomer might refer to somebody who's been here for a hundred years.

"So you're thinking about whether or not you want to enter the competition," he said, looking directly into the camera. "You've probably guessed by now that I'm a past winner. Correction. That was a silly thing to say. Because if you win this competition, you've won for life.

"I've been where you are." He grinned. "I got buffalo

wildwings with six dipping sauces and two racks of ribs for supper. No matter what you're feelin' right now, you couldn't possibly be feelin' more out of place than I did.

"So you get the idea. We're not all the same. Far from it. I'm guessing some of you are having dishes I couldn't spell or even pronounce. In the end, it's not so much about who you are as whether or not you're right for the debutantes. There are two this year."

As he continued to walk slowly the background scenery changed slightly and every new view seemed to be more enchanting than the last.

"You probably wouldn't think I'd be a candidate for something like this. I was an outlaw biker who got sucked into that life on a promise of fun, anarchy, and pussy.

"After eight years what I had to show for it was this." He grabbed the neckline of the knit shirt and tugged it down to reveal an angry-looking red slash across his chest. "Let me tell you, it's not fun to get shot at or knifed. It's not anarchy when you have to follow somebody else's orders twenty-four-seven, right or not, like it or not. And the pussy? Christ. Looking back I can't believe the nasty cunts I stuck my dick into.

"I wanted out, but there was no walking away. Except for this. Thank the gods for this. It saved my life.

"Now I fish for catfish." He looked over his shoulder at the river behind him. "They're some monsters in there. I take 'em home, somebody else cleans 'em up, covers 'em in corn meal like they ought to be, and fries 'em up.

"I ride my Harley through the hills when I get restless. The Hill Country is the best ride anywhere. Guaranteed to clear your head and make you glad you're alive. Sometimes I go climbing over at Canyon Lake Gorge. I kayak on the Comal River when we get a flood. If the rapids don't get your heart goin' then you're not alive. My wife doesn't like it when I do that stuff, but…" he shrugged and grinned, "you know.

"The last part is the best. My wife. I'm not going into that. All I'll say about it is this. Get your own.

"That's what you have a chance to do."

Wait. What?!?

There're no guarantees. Two weeks from now about fifty guys will show up here in Wimberley with big dreams, but only two will ring the bell and snuff out the candle."

Ring the bell and snuff out the candle?

"The other forty-eight will go home not remembering what they saw and heard, wondering why the fuck they went to Wimberley of all places." He chuckled. "It's better for everybody that way.

"So enjoy your dinner. If you decide to go on to the next step and you pass the test, I'll see you here. Otherwise, hasta la vista, baby."

As the image faded, the lights came up slightly and the acoustic guitar music resumed. The wait staff hurried to remove the remains of our first course, replace it with the entrée we all wanted, but didn't choose, and refill the wine.

Charlie got prime rib. Robert got sea bass. Ivan got lamb lollypops with mint sauce. Harper got lobster. After seeing these expensive delicacies delivered to my peers, I laughed out loud when I was presented with tomato-sauce covered meatloaf. I don't know how they got my mother's recipe, but by damn, that was what I wanted more than anything else at that moment in time. I just hadn't known it until they put it in front of me.

The other guys looked at me and my plate when I laughed out loud. The waiter looked worried. "Is everything alright, Mr. Draiocht?"

"Oh yeah," I said. "It's beyond perfect."

As soon as everyone was served, the wait staff withdrew, the guitar music faded, and the screen lit again. This time the camera was focused on a guy returning tennis balls as fast as the ball machine launched them his way. He wore new-style bright tennis clothes and had a red bandana tied on his head. When the ball machine stopped, he jogged over to a mark in front of the camera.

The tennis court was set high on a hill with a two-hundred-seventy-degree view.

"I'm Stefan," he said with an accent that suggested Eastern European.

The guy looked to be taller than average, but he had a tennis build, strong and wiry. His tan looked like he spent a lot of time on the court and his dark hair and eyes reminded me a little of Rafael Nadal.

"I was a winner seven years ago." He looked over his shoulder. "I like playing, but I didn't like the stress or politics of the pro circuit. Now I play for fun and teach kids. You'd have to be a lunatic to ask if I have regrets."

The camera moved backward as Stefan walked forward. "Is it Camelot here? I guess that depends on what Camelot is to you." He climbed a set of wide stone steps to another level opening onto an infinity pool with an even more spectacular view. "Everybody has their own idea of what that means."

As Stefan turned, the camera turned with him so that he was backed by a view of a breathtaking white columned Grecian-style villa, three stories high with flagstone patios, bronze statues of deer, and filmy gauze drapes on the veranda. It was probably the most romantic thing I'd ever seen. What I mean is, I would probably think so if I was a woman.

Stefan's arm swept behind him to encompass the building. He smiled like the cat who got the canary and said, "But this is pretty good."

I had to agree with Stefan. The promise of life like that is what turns people to crime.

As Stefan's smile faded from view, the image was replaced with a set of wide iron gates bearing the same WW crest I'd seen all around the building in which I was presently having dinner.

A female narrator with a velvety, seductive voice said, "This is the entrance to our little colony. Of course access is invitation-only." As the camera panned up, we saw that there were quite a few white palaces dotting hilltops and hillsides. "Residents are encouraged to pursue whatever interest is at the center of their heart's desire. While you're finishing dinner, we'll give you a taste of local life in Wimberley. It's not just for us, you know. It's also an artists' colony."

Strains of acoustic guitar returned to create audio backing for a video of galleries. Each showed people viewing paintings or sculptures, conversing with the artists, or negotiating terms for purchase.

It would have been really interesting, an artists' colony in an area as remote as Wimberley, but the video suggested they draw enough visitors from San Antonio and Austin, or elsewhere, to keep them thriving.

If I was fitting the puzzle pieces together correctly, this was some kind of contest of would-be suitors. The winners would, apparently, spend the rest of their days kept in the lap of luxury by sugar mamas. In exchange for what? Being sex slaves to somebody who had to go to these lengths to find a man? I would say I was about to hit rock bottom, but that would be hard to sell from a hilltop Grecian palace with all the time I wanted to do whatever.

The video faded to black, the lights and music came up a little and the wait staff rushed out to make sure we were treated like kings, removing dinner plates to make room for dessert.

"What else can we get you, Mr. Draiocht? Coffee? Bananas Foster?"

I smiled. At that point it didn't surprise me that they knew I had a place in my stomach in permanent reserve for the next offer of Bananas Foster. "Now how could I refuse an offer like that?"

My waiter's brown eyes gleamed. "It will be right out, sir."

I nodded. "Thank you."

I heard the other 'contestants' agreeing to similar offers. All except for Robert who declined while making a rather loud statement about love handles and the evils of sugar. If you'd have asked me which of the four would be that asshole, I would have pointed at him an hour ago and said, "Yep. That's the one. No question." He was just wearing that holier-than-thou smarminess like a gooey aura.

While we waited for a selection of the world's best desserts, three of us were poured coffee from individual silver carafes that were left sitting at our place just in case we wanted self-serve seconds.

The waiter lifted the little pitcher of cream, "Shall I pour, Mr. Draiocht?"

"No. I prefer doctoring my own coffee. Thank you for the brown sugar. Nice touch."

My waiter looked a little shocked that he was being thanked for condiments. "You're welcome, sir. Would you care for more?"

I looked from him to the Sterling sugar bowl holding enough brown sugar for six months. "This will do." I leaned forward, lowered my voice in conspiracy. "And I wouldn't want to offend the sugar police."

My waiter, who had apparently heard Robert's rant, snorted.

After stirring with a dainty demitasse spoon... I know what it is because my mother collects them and hangs them on the wall, I lifted the cup to my lips and took a sip. I barely managed to suppress the kind of moan that comes from getting really, really good head. The coffee was so good I thought I'd been transported to nirvana.

"Oh, man," I said, turning to Harper. "This coffee is good."

"Nothing but the best for the witches," he confirmed.

"You know, I get the feeling that everybody here knows more than I do. I more or less did this on a whim. A guy gave me a mysterious card. Anyway, this is about mail-order husbands or something like that?"

He grinned and shook his head. "It's more like winning the lottery. You get picked by one of the witches. You're set for life."

"Okay. Now when you say witches, what do you…?"

Desserts were being served, mine with some extra flamboyance, heavy on the first syllable since they actually lit it on fire. They did a beautiful job of it, just enough brandy to cause a show without singeing eyebrows off or making torches of tablecloths.

Again the lights went down and the music came up.

We were looking at a guy sitting in a high tech music recording studio that would have put the MIT band, Boston, to shame. He was holding a guitar that even I recognized as a vintage Gibson, fifties Les Paul. I almost whistled because I knew that it would cost more than ten thousand dollars if you could find one for sale. They normally only came up as auction items at charity events for the super-rich.

Anyway the guy was sitting on a stool, in front of a mic. He was what you'd call average-looking. His hair was curling over his ears. He was wearing a bright floral Hawaiian shirt and Buddy Holly glasses.

"I'm Simon," he said, reaching up to push his glasses up the bridge of his nose. "I think they picked me to be in this promo video thing just to show that winners are no particular type. You don't know what they're looking for until they pick.

"That should be comforting. Means you can relax." He looked down at his guitar and strummed a riff almost like it was a nervous habit or like he was used to having the guitar talk for him.

"I'm a songwriter and an introvert, in that order. I'm not interested in going on tour or playing in front of people. I just like writing songs for other people who want that.

"That's who I've been all my life. So what's the difference between now and before? Now my songs find their way into the hands of stars. They get copyrighted and recorded and appreciated by millions of people."

He looked down, played a riff, then pushed his glasses up, looked at the camera and said, "So that's cool. Right?"

Well, yeah, I had to agree with Simon's assessment. It *was* cool. What he got was a lot better than a lottery win. He got the world on Simon's terms.

"If you pass the preliminary test, all you've got to lose is a four-day-weekend. You know? So maybe I'll see you around here." He played another riff then smiled at the camera shyly. "That's all I got."

The lights came up to pre-dinner candlepower, the cabinetry that hid the screen whirred closed, and Ms. Blackwell entered as if on cue.

"As you've seen, gentlemen, there's not a particular type of person who's more likely to be selected than another. Your destiny is up to, well, destiny. If you choose to move forward, we'll schedule some testing to be conducted here over the next few days. Those who pass will be invited to Wimberley for a long weekend that could change your life dramatically.

"Which of you would like to move forward?"

The other four raised their hands immediately. I raised my hand reluctantly, but said, "I have a question."

Blackwell smiled. "Mr. Draiocht. I might have guessed."

I didn't know what that meant, but I forged ahead. "Is there something binding in an agreement to 'move forward'?"

She grinned. "Binding? An interesting choice of words. No. Winners are presented offers in contract form. Those who accept the contract obligate themselves to a year. The option to terminate can be exercised by either suitor or prize before midnight on the last day of the first year together. Does that answer your question?"

"Yes," I said, although my mind was a maelstrom of questions.

"Are you in or out?" she asked me point blank.

"In," I said, feeling a little like I'd been called out by my homeroom teacher.

THE TESTING WAS partly physical and mostly psychic, especially of interest to me since that was my interest. On Friday I was told that I was eligible to make arrangements to be in Wimberley, that I needed to arrive on Wednesday and leave on Sunday.

Before I could voice the question, Blackwell said, "Yes, Mr. Draiocht, you will be given a travel allowance that should cover reasonable expenses."

I smiled big. "Sweet."

My travel allowance came in the form of a credit card in my name. Seeing the look on my face, she said, "*Reasonable* expenses, Mr. Draiocht. If you have visions of being a big spender then you need to not only go, but win."

"I'll do my best, Ms. Blackwell. If it doesn't work out then maybe you'd be interested in a burger by the beach?"

She laughed. "You are unique, Mr. Draiocht. Just the sort who might actually stand a chance." She shook her head. "The answer is no. I don't date contestants. Ever. So don't take it personally."

I shrugged and gave her a half grin. "Okay. But your loss."

"No doubt. Besides, Mr. Draiocht, you may meet your true love. Don't be sure it's not going to work out before you're even on the plane to Austin."

"Austin?"

"Closest airport."

"Oh."

"And don't forget to make a hotel reservation. They hold enough rooms for contestants, but some of them are outside town."

Nodding, I said, "Thanks for the tip."

"Good luck."

chapter three

T HAT BRINGS US back to why I'm here in Wimberley, staying at the ghost hotel. There's some kind of barbeque down at the river tonight. Some of the other contestants told me it's one of the "sorcials". That's a play on the word sorcery. I'm a little bit bothered by that because I'm no closer to finding out why these people call themselves witches.

There's this meet-and-greet thing tonight and then the Witches' Ball, the big to-do, tomorrow night. I'm going through the motions, but not committing to anything. What keeps going through my head is, could I even get it up for a woman who has to go to these lengths to get laid?

One thing at a time.

That thing Blackwell said, about true love… if that's the goal, then I'm sore out of luck. I don't believe in love, much less 'true love'. I'm here because I wouldn't mind spending a year on an all-expense-paid luxury vacay with nothing to do but be lazy. Well, that, and possibly service a woman I couldn't look at. Even that didn't discourage me though. That's what light switches are for. Right?

I'm still curious about the whole 'witch' thing. Why would people want to self-identify as witches, especially in the part of Texas where everybody has wrought iron longhorns and a welded Texas star decorating their property?

I STEPPED OUT on the decking that forms a wooden sidewalk in front of the hotel thinking I'd take a walk around town, maybe see some of those galleries that were in the presentation.

Two old guys with beards were sitting in rockers to the side. It was so nineteenth century that I wondered if they were paid to be props. Turning east, I saw a little girl, about eight years old, rollerblading toward me. She stopped in the street in front of me and looked up.

"Are you lost?" I asked. She shook her head. "Should you be out here all by yourself?" She laughed at that and the sound made me think of tinkling wind chimes.

"You must not be from around here," said one of the old guys just before he turned and spat chew into a brass spittoon.

"No. I'm not," I said, trying not to look disgusted by the spittle.

The guy pointed two fingers at the little girl and smiled. "She's one of 'em."

The child looked back up at me. "I'm Destiny. Some people leave off the Des and call me Tiny, but I don't like that. I may be tiny, but it's temporary."

"Temporary is a big word for someone your age."

She shrugged. "I'm smart."

"Well, I can tell."

"What's your name?"

For some reason that I couldn't name in a hundred years, I opened my mouth to say 'Will', but what came out was, "Willem."

She grinned with teeth spread wide apart for growing into. "I like that. My sister is coming out. I'll tell her to look for you. Maybe you'll be in my family."

"Maybe I'll just wait for you," I teased. "Maybe you're my destiny."

Her giggles were bar none the most charming thing I'd ever seen on a female person of any age. Her curls bounced a little as she shook her head. "You're not for me, Willem. But I wish you were. Bye." She waved goodbye. For a second I thought she would skate away, but something stopped her.

Looking back in the direction she'd come from I saw that there was an enormous black bear loping down the middle of the street.

As it happened the hotel was built at the intersection of a crossroads that in modern times had taken the form of a ninety degree turn. A car came careening around the curve going way too fast for a little touristy town. I watched in horror as the bear reared up on his hind legs and roared at the car, which was one second away from crashing into him.

"Nooooooo," said Destiny. She held her little palms up toward the impending horror and pushed as if she was pushing against something heavy in the air.

I don't expect you to believe what happened next. Why would you? I barely believe it and I was there.

The bear vanished from the road where he was about

to roar his last roar. As soon as that transpired a beagle appeared at Destiny's feet, looking shame-faced.

"Izobath! You've been a very, very, very bad beagle." She shook her finger at the dog, who was looking like the living definition of a hang-dog expression. "Go home right now and don't you dare think about stepping into the street again."

The dog slunk away with his tail between his legs.

When he was gone, she smiled at me. "Izzy has a bear fantasy."

I was too stunned for my mind to be functioning properly so, rather than ask what I really wanted to know, I said, "Izobath is a really unusual name for a dog."

She giggled. "Raider found him wandering around when he was a puppy and brought him home. Ruby, she's a friend of my sister's, can hear what animals say. Izzy told her his name was Izobath."

"How did he do that? It seems like a mouthful for a dog."

She giggled again. "Well he didn't say it out loud, silly. He said it in his mind."

I nodded. "So Ruby who can read animals' minds."

She shook her head. "Not just animals."

"Thanks for the warning."

"Okay," she said. "See ya."

She skated away.

I looked at the two old guys who had witnessed the entire event. They might have been statues except for the rocking of the chairs and the twinkle in their eyes. And the fact that I'd heard one of them speak in a semi-appropriate manner.

"Did you see a bear?" I asked.

"Did you?" The one on the right leaned over and spit.

"So you're gonna play it like that."

"I saw a beagle that'd run away from home. Had no business bein' in the street."

"Okay. Whatever."

I spent a few hours wandering through the galleries. Some of them were eclectic. There'd be a matte black and white photo of Billy Gibbons of ZZ Top right next to a twenty-five-thousand-dollar oil painting of a cattle drive.

If I'd had the money I would have bought a portrait of a woman with long black hair, pale green eyes, and red lips to match the dress she was wearing. I was debating whether I wanted to ask the gallery owner if I could work off the cost of the painting. I turned to look for him, but he was talking with someone about a modern iron sculpture. When I looked back to the painting, it was of an old guy in a sailor suit.

After blinking a couple of times, it was still an old guy in a sailor suit. The plaque read Captain King with a subtitle King Ranch. Just to see what would happen I looked away and then back a few times, but the old codger held firm and refused to give up the haunting vision of the green-eyed woman.

"What's the matter?"

I jumped when the owner sneaked up behind me.

"Nothing," I said. "What do you mean?"

"Well, you've been standing here so long, I thought perhaps you'd seen the portrait of Pleasant Wimberley."

He must have caught something passing over my face that gave me away. "Ah, you have then. I, myself, have never been fortunate enough to see her occupy someone else's visage, but I've been told you never forget it."

Looking from him to the portrait and back again, I said, "Are you suggesting that I witnessed a paranormal event?"

He chuckled. "That's a fancy modern way of describing it, but sure."

"Tell me what you know about this."

The bell that hung from the door jingled as three new customers came in. "Be right with you," he said to them.

Lowering his voice, he said to me, "You saw the founder of the town, Pleasant Wimberley. She likes to prank the tourists by showing up in other people's portraits. I've heard she's really something to look at. I've also noticed she only does it to people who can handle experiencing a supernatural occurrence without going nuts about it."

I nodded. "I wanted the painting so bad, I was going to ask you if I could work off whatever it cost."

He laughed. "That's a new one. I'll bet she loved hearing that. Have a nice stay in Wimberley."

With that he walked toward the new arrivals.

After looking at the portrait one more time, just couldn't help myself, I walked two blocks up to the tavern. The calling card was the smell of charcoal-broiled hamburger and French fries, which carries for about a block around, and made me instantly ravenous.

It was early afternoon, but the place was still busy. I

saw an open seat at the counter and headed in that direction. It didn't take a genius to figure out that the other guys sitting at the bar were also contestants. I noticed Ivan and gave him a chin lift.

I ordered the burger basket with cheese, hickory sauce, a mix of plain and sweet potato fries and a Lonestar beer.

The guy next to me said, "You're not going to have that physique for long eating like that."

Looking him up and down, I went out of my way to be dismissive. Honestly, I'd never had a stranger comment openly about my 'physique' except in auditions.

"May the best man win," I said.

I held up my longneck Lonestar beer. He held up his longneck IBC rootbeer. When we clinked bottles, he said, "Yeah. The best man. I'm Roger."

"Willem," I replied, having apparently lost the ability to make my tongue form the name 'Will'.

"You going to the barbeque?"

"Came all the way from L.A. So, yeah. I'm gonna see where this leads."

"L.A.?" he said. "I took you for a southerner."

"Why's that?"

"Don't know. Just thought I heard it in your speech."

After all the time, money and energy I'd spent getting rid of my accent, this wasn't something I wanted to hear from Roger. Less than a day in Texas shouldn't undo ten years of diction lessons.

"Where're you from, Roger?"

"Minnesota."

I laughed out loud. "That would be quite an adjustment, if you won. I mean I think it gets down to fifty degrees once or twice a year here."

We chatted more or less amiably until my food came. I cut the burger in half. I wouldn't have been surprised if there wasn't a half pound of meat, done to perfection. I scarfed an Idaho fry, then a sweet potato fry, then bit into hickory cheeseburger heaven on Earth.

"Oh, man," I said with my mouth half full. "I could eat here every day for the rest of my life and never get tired of this."

Roger smirked. "So what's your special talent?"

"Special talent?" I repeated stupidly.

"Yes. You weren't just picked from the phone book at random. You know that, right?"

"Well," I hesitated with burger heaven suspended just an inch from my mouth, "I hadn't really thought about it. Maybe on some level?"

"Some level. Wow. What are you even doing here?"

"Heard the gig is a prize beyond compare."

"Yeah," he said, studying me. "That it is. So what do you do? For a living, I mean."

"Out of work actor."

"Really. Surprising. You're good-looking enough to be in the movies."

"That's what I've been told by people who aren't offering paying acting jobs."

"Hmmm. Bummer."

"How about you?"

"Roofer."

"Roofer in Minnesota? You must have a lot of free

time."

"Really busy in the summer. Snow does a lot of damage to roofs. But I do have time for ice fishing."

"So what brings you to this, ah, competition?"

"Roofing is rough. The work is so awful you can't get anybody to do it except ex-cons and the only reason why they take the work is because nobody else will hire them. And let me tell you. There's a reason why nobody else will hire them. If they had a work ethic, they wouldn't have sought out a life of crime."

"I can see that. So if you won, what would you do with your time?" I more or less repeated Blackwell's question to me. He shook his head and looked embarrassed. "Come on. I won't judge you."

"I like orchids."

"What?" I did my best to keep a straight face.

"You said no judging."

"I'm not judging. I just, never mind."

"I want to develop a new species that blooms longer."

"Where did you go to Orientation?"

"Chicago."

"Did they mention 'heart's desire'?"

"Something like that."

"So that's your heart's desire. If you had free time and money wasn't an issue, you'd fool around with flowers?"

He grinned and nodded. "Yeah."

"Well then, Roger. I hope you get the other spot."

"If I don't, I'm gonna be glad they wiped my memory 'cause I wouldn't want to spend the rest of my life thinking that I might have been coaxing new orchids in a greenhouse instead of babysitting criminals on roofs."

"I heard something about the memory wipe thing, but I didn't think they meant that literally. I mean that can't really be done, can it?"

He squinted his eyes and gave me a little smile like he questioned *my* sanity.

"You *do* know we're talking about witches, right?"

"I know there are a lot of people who call themselves witches, but what it means is they like burning candles and herbs, dancing naked in some cases, I guess. Are you saying you think there are women here who really are touched by the supernatural?"

He laughed. "Man. I don't know how you're sitting on that stool next to me. How did you manage to get this far without knowing anything about what you're doing here?" He shook his head. "Yes. I mean there are women here who really are touched by the supernatural."

I had to admit that I felt a thrill start in my nipples and run all the way through my body, producing goosebumps, a cock twitch, and a half hard. What if it was true? I'd spent my whole life secretly hoping that I'd be lucky enough to have an actual encounter with the other side of reality, while not really believing that such a thing might be possible.

That's when I realized that I'd been on the wrong path. For the first time I recognized and confronted the fact that I didn't really want to be an actor. I hadn't wanted to be a college student taking a foreign language I would never use or studying geology, which I would never use. But I hadn't really wanted to be an actor either. It was just

Plan B more or less suggested by other people. My heart wasn't in it at all.

Acting as my heart's desire? Don't make me laugh. Actually there's not much laughable about wasting ten years pursuing something I didn't even want.

That revelation made me feel like the dumbest guy sitting on a counter stool anywhere. Why hadn't I clued in before? And what if I couldn't get jobs acting because I wasn't *supposed* to be acting?

That follow-up insight almost blew me right off the stool.

"If that's true, it would be beyond incredible."

"You scared?"

It hadn't occurred to me to be scared before and maybe that just meant I was revealing an infinite capacity for stupidity.

"Should I be?" He shrugged. "Do you believe there's a ghost at the hotel, too?"

Roger laughed again. He had a nice laugh. I wondered if that's what they were looking for. All of a sudden I found myself seriously caring about what they were looking for.

I wasn't interested in contemplating a lifetime contract of marriage, but I could do a year with anybody if it meant doing actual hands-on research. Maybe I should say on-site research.

He lifted a well-toned shoulder. "Who knows? I can't say I've seen anything like that, but ley lines intersect at the crossroads."

I jerked my gaze back to his. "Ley lines? You know

about ley lines?"

"I know enough."

Deciding to let that go, I said, "So we're going to meet the witches at the barbeque tonight?"

He shook his head while still taking a pull on his IBC. When he'd swallowed he said, "I think it's just contestants and former winners. Our chance to talk to them about life in Wimberley or whatever. They'll be at the big event tomorrow night though. The Witches' Ball."

The first time I'd heard that phrase it hadn't made an impression on me, but this time it registered that balls usually mean formal dress. I was kind of alarmed by that.

While signing the credit card slip for my burger and beer, I said, "Hey, for the, ah, Witches' Ball, has a suggestion been made about how to dress?"

"I think they're pretty casual, big on letting people do their own thing."

If Roger wasn't competing for one of two places, I would have felt secure with that answer, but as it stood, I wasn't sure I could trust it. And I didn't want to be the only guy in jeans while everybody else was in ball gowns and monkey suits. On the other hand, maybe individuality was what they were looking for?

It wasn't hard to see that I could go crazy with circular arguments. So I decided to ask around at the barbeque. If I needed a tux, I'd manage to get to either Austin or San Antonio and score black tie before tomorrow night.

There was one crispy fry left at the bottom of the basket. It looked too good to go to waste. So I popped it in my mouth to join the party going on in my happy tummy and slid off the stool.

"See you tonight," Roger said.

"Yep," I replied and headed for the door.

Wimberley couldn't possibly be more different from L.A. It moved as slow as molasses. A lot of people would say that like it was a bad thing, but you know what moves even slower than molasses? L.A. freeways. Big city life isn't all that.

I strolled back to the hotel, grabbed a newspaper from the stack at the front desk, and sat down in the lobby. Seemed like a good way to get a jump on checking out the competition.

It wasn't hard to recognize my opponents. They were all guys in their twenties and, while I knew from the video that outstanding looks weren't necessarily a requirement, all the suitors I'd seen in person would definitely be called "hot" by the women I know.

As they came and went from the hotel, their eyes would invariably fall on me sitting there looking over the top of a newspaper. Seemed we were all doing the same thing, trying to check out the competition, look for weaknesses, some way to eke out an edge over the next guy.

After an hour of that I found myself thinking, "What's vacation for if not naps?"

So I left the paper on the heavy wood and wrought iron coffee table and went upstairs. Before calling the number on the card I was pretty sure I hadn't had a nap since the time when naps came with milk and cookies. Now I was about to rack up my second in a week. I stretched out on the bed and waited to see what would happen.

I must have fallen asleep pretty soon after that. When I woke, it was five o'clock, which coincidentally was the same time as the barbeque. *Shit.* I was making a habit of almost missing important events because of over-napping.

After throwing water in my face and running my hands through my hair a couple of times, I raced down the steps and out the front door. Fortunately it was a two minute jog. I knew where to go because I'd seen them setting up for it earlier in the day. There was a quaint-looking café that had access to the grassy river bank below, access that could be denied if you weren't expected.

The entrance was being guarded by a djin. At least that was my first thought when I saw the enormous black guy with his shiny bald head and single gold earring. As I approached he gave me a big smile, said, "Good evening, Mr. Draiocht," and opened the picket gate for me to pass through. "Glad you could make it. Just go down the steps. Everybody's down by the river."

I could hear that. A crowd of all men using conversational tones produces a distinct low rumble.

"Thank you," I said, knowing it was an appropriate response but thinking it sounded lame anyway.

Following the sound of voices, I rushed through the café courtyard and down the steps. Several tents were set up in case of rain, but it was a nice night. In fact, it was a perfect night. Seventy degrees that would become sixty-eight when the sun went down. No wind. No insects. Just enough humidity to soften the air and keep my eyes from trying to wither away in my own head as they sometimes did in L.A's dry air.

As I took the last three steps I was thinking that maybe Wimberley was heaven.

A few people looked over and visibly noted my tardiness. I supposed I was the only one who was late, but I've got to tell you, that nap was good.

I spotted Ivan. When I caught his eye, he gave me a friendly chin lift so I began moving in his direction to say hello. Before I reached him I was intercepted by a waiter.

"What can I get you to drink, Mr. Draiocht?"

"Margarita."

"Very good, sir. Would you like frozen or on the rocks?"

"Rocks."

"Salt or no salt?"

"No salt."

"Would you like that with 1800, Hornitos, or we stock four kinds of Jose Cuervo: Gold, Silver Especial, Tradicional Reposado, and Extra Anejo."

"Reposado."

He smiled, gave a tiny head nod and disappeared.

Ivan smiled. He'd watched the whole exchange. "What is it with you and complicated drinks?"

"Seems they take their margaritas as seriously as I do."

"Will," he said, "this is Kellan."

"Kellan," I repeated as I shook his hand. Looking around I said, "So this is the competition."

"Well, no. About fifteen of these guys are winners."

"Other than the ones from the video, how do you

know who's who?"

Ivan shrugged.

Kellan said, "The older ones are probably winners."

"Yeah," said Ivan, "but just to be on the safe side I'm going to ask before I start talking."

"Makes sense. If they tell the truth." Turning back to Kellan, I said, "Winner or wannabe?"

He laughed, clearly surprised. "Good one."

I smiled. "Thanks. But you didn't answer the question."

His grin resolved into a smile as he studied me with sparkling eyes. "Okay. You got me. I'm a winner. Been here for six years."

Truthfully? I wasn't expecting that. Partly because I wasn't expecting the winners to be pretending to be contestants. I guess they were bound to tell the truth when asked point blank though. Good to know.

"So, Kellan. What's your heart's desire?"

He laughed again. "You're a fast learner, Willem."

I cocked my head to the side. "How did you know my birth name is Willem?"

"You're a fast learner, but if you win, you'll find you've got a lot to learn. Later." He walked away, smiling like somebody who had the best secret in the universe.

"Wow," Ivan said, looking a little stunned.

"You didn't say anything incriminating, did you?"

Ivan looked worried. He seemed to be sifting back through their conversation. "I don't think so. I just thought he was an amiable sort."

"He probably is. Winners don't have to be assholes. At

least I don't think so. The guys on the video seemed genuine enough."

"Yeah. They did. Especially the musician."

"Simon?"

"That's the one."

"Wonder if he's here. I think he'd be most likely to give up juicy info."

Ivan nodded. "Let's hunt him down."

Something about the way he said that brought out the predator in me. So I responded with what I thought was a manly nod and let my eyes wander over the gathering.

A tray appeared in front of my line of sight. "One margarita, Mr. Draiocht. On the rocks, no salt, Jose Reposado."

The margarita was presented in a heavy Mexican blown glass goblet that could have come from one of the local galleries, and probably did. I took a sip and let my eyes go closed. Damn. I couldn't make myself a margarita that good.

"Anything else, sir?"

"This is perfection, …?"

I let the question hang in the air making it clear that I was asking for his name.

"Roque. Quintanilla." He added his surname as an afterthought.

"Thank you for the best margarita I've ever had, Mister Quintanilla."

He nodded and disappeared into the crowd with a grin on his face.

We began skirting around the edges of the crowd for

signs of Simon, but I suspected that everyone there was taller than our target. In the end it turned out that he was even shorter than the space in the air where I'd been looking, because he was sitting down at a long raised table in the big tent. Alone. With something that looked like a Tequila Sunrise, a little too colorful for guys' night out if you ask me.

The table had chairs on only one side, like the Last Supper, so we went around the ends, each of us approaching him from opposite ends.

"Hey, Simon," I said as we approached.

As I pulled out the chair next to him, he said, "This table isn't for contestants. Contestants sit out there." He gestured to the rest of the room.

"Okay. Well, we'll leave when the party moves in here."

I looked over at Ivan meaningfully. He said, "Yes. Soon as they start this way, we're ghosts."

Simon barked out a laugh that made him seem a little looney. He pushed his glasses up his nose.

"So," I said. "We saw you in the video."

His eyes slanted toward me with suspicion. "Yeah?"

"Yeah. So I don't have to ask about your heart's desire. You didn't tell us what kind of music you write."

He snorted. "You don't care about music."

"The hell you say!" I exclaimed, hearing that Alabama was creeping back into my speech with or without permission. I supposed that twenty-four hours of hearing Texas drawl was involuntarily extending my vowels and softening my consonants. "I know enough to know that was a five figure Gibson Les Paul you were fondling."

His eyes widened just a little. He pushed his glasses up his nose, gave me a small smile, and glanced at Ivan, perhaps to see what he was up to.

"Not everybody would know that."

"Damn straight."

He looked curious. "You from around here?"

"No. Why?"

"Just your, uh, terminology. And your cadence. It's more harmonic in the South. And in Texas. Although Texas is technically the Southwest."

"Alabama," I said. It had been a while since I'd felt pride in saying that and, by God, it felt good.

He grinned. "Sweet Home."

"Amen."

He chuckled. I had him.

"You gonna tell me what kind of music you're writin'?"

"Here's the thing, when times change music gets relabeled. I'm doing something that's not rock and not country, but a little bit of both."

"Like Rockabilly."

"No. No. No," he said. "Not like that at all." He slanted his eyes toward me. "Do you really know what Rockabilly is?"

I shrugged. "Of course. Buddy Holly, Jerry Lee Lewis, Carl Perkins. And, don't hate me for this, but Stray Cats."

That got me a huge grin. He banged the table with the palm of his hand. "Hah! Stray Cats. They did fifties better than anybody in the fifties did fifties!"

I held my palm up for a high five and said, "My man!"

As Simon slapped my hand I allowed a quick glance at Ivan who was sitting back, enjoying the exchange and grinning like a Cheshire cat.

"Okay, so you know Rockabilly," Simon began. "I like songs that tell a story. Like The Eagles. You know at one time they were considered rock. A couple of decades went by and then they were reclassified as soft rock. Another decade went by and they were being covered by every country singer who had a say in what went on albums." I nodded encouragingly. "I think what they were doing is timeless."

"So you're reviving the sound."

"Maybe," he said with a new coyness. "That's the goal."

"Thing about The Eagles sound… the songs and the musicianship were flawless, but it was all about the harmonies. They used to say the Beach Boys were pioneers of harmony and they were settlers."

He was nodding excitedly. "True, but I'm not a copy-cat. I'm creating something original. I'm just saying that Eagles were a big influence."

"Gotcha. Well, if one of us wins, we're gonna be banging on your studio door and demanding a private performance."

He gave us both a small smile. "Maybe."

"So, Simon, we keep hearing that there's nothing we can do to prepare, no way to get an edge on the competition. That true?"

He nodded. "That's true. You're either it or you're

not." As soon as he said it, he blanched, eyes going wide like he'd said something he wasn't supposed to say. He stammered a little, trying to recover. "Look, there's really nothing to tell. No way to game the outcome if that's what you're looking for."

"Just tell me one thing. What are we supposed to wear to the thing tomorrow night?"

He chuckled. "I'll bet somebody's already told you it doesn't matter and I'll bet you didn't believe them."

Nodding, I said, "Maybe."

"Believe it. Wear whatever you want. It won't matter one way or the other. Winners aren't chosen because of style. If they were, I certainly wouldn't be sitting at this table."

I held out my hand to shake his. "Thanks, man. Enjoyed the chat."

Simon shook my hand. Ivan and I stood up just as people were filing in to be seated for dinner. "Later."

As I rounded the end of the table to find a seat, he called after me. "I hope you win!"

I grinned and gave him a thumbs-up.

"Since we're already right in front of the head table, let's snag two chairs."

I nodded. "Back of the class never wins."

"Exactly what I was thinking. Lucky you knew that music stuff."

"Why? It didn't get us any new info."

"Disagree. I, for one, will feel okay about whatever I wear tomorrow night knowing clothes have nothing to do with winning." He pulled out a chair. "How'd you know all that stuff anyway?"

"My dad is an aficionado. He converted the garage into a room that might as well be a guitar museum. He plays, but never got the chance to try to do it professionally. Family came along when he was young. Luckily for us he was more serious about responsibility than heart's desire."

As soon as I'd said that out loud the phrase heart's desire resonated through my mind like a bone-deep vibration. I'd never thought much about heart's desire before, but now that it was part of my consciousness, seemed like I couldn't think of anything else. My dad would have *loved* to play music for work. Maybe he would have liked to be Simon. I don't know.

We were sitting in the two premier seats front and center, like eager geeks in calculus, waiting to see what would happen next. We watched the winners file in, greet each other, and take their seats. Good old Kellan stood at the centermost chair and gave the appearance of someone in charge.

When everyone was seated, he tapped his glass with a spoon. The noise didn't die down gradually. Silence was abrupt.

"Dinner is about to be served, gentlemen. Don't expect tailor-made menus like what you enjoyed at Orientation. This is local fare, but I expect you'll like it. Don't be shy. Eat as much as you want. The witches have made this a calorie-free zone for tonight. No amount of fat, salt, or sugar will have any effect on your girlish figures."

Immediately I heard murmurs behind me, guys turning to each other and asking, "Do you think he's serious? Is it really a calorie-free zone? Can they do that?"

I turned back toward the dais. Kellan looked down at me sitting right in front of him and winked, which of course left me agonizing over whether that was a good wink or a bad wink and trying to dissect whether or not there was any such thing as a 'bad wink'. Then I started thinking the wink might have been indicating that the calorie-free thing was a joke. God. I wished he hadn't winked.

Kellan continued. "While the food is being passed around, I'm going to kick things off by officially welcoming you to Win a Witch Weekend. I hope you've had a chance to look around Wimberley. It's not New York and we like it that way." The guys on the dais all clapped and nodded in agreement so, naturally, the contestants followed suit.

I had to admit the guys on the platform all seemed relaxed and pleased to be winners. I guessed from the Win a Witch Weekend reference that meant that each of them had won his own witch. And since none of them seemed to be blind, that meant it had turned out okay. I guess it would have turned out okay if they *were* blind, but you know what I mean.

"Wimberley is a special place for special people," Kellan went on. "That's why artists are pulled here like there's a creative vortex at work. We even have a few winners who are into the arts." He looked down the table. "Like Simon over there, whom you saw in the Orientation video."

Simon didn't smile or wave or stand up and take a

bow, but he did push his glasses up the bridge of his nose.

"Winners are as diverse as the people you'd find on any street corner."

I looked around and thought, *Yeah. On the street corner where the convention for models and rugby players just broke for lunch.*

"As you know, the ball is tomorrow night. By the time the clock strikes twelve, you'll know if you're one of the very lucky few to be welcomed into this brotherhood." I heard the murmur of voices behind me, but they were silenced as soon as Kellan began speaking again. "Regardless of the outcome, we want you to have a good time while you're here. So after dinner you're invited to sign up for one of the activities we're sponsoring tomorrow during the day."

The room filled with wait staff and heavenly aromas as platters of Texas barbeque and sides filled the room. Each person carried something different, stopped in front of us with a serving spoon, ladle, or meat fork depending on what they presented, and allowed us to serve ourselves. In order of appearance, if I remember correctly, was beef brisket, turkey breast, fresh pork, barbeque sauce, potato salad, green salad, macaroni in white cheese, pinto beans, corn on the cob, jalapeno cornbread and/or warm butter rolls.

Since there was no longer any danger of my abs ever being scrutinized by a camera close-up, I took some of everything. That was a feat even considering that they gave us platters instead of plates. I looked behind me. There were a whole lot of happy, happy guys. Maybe that whole thing about the way to a man's heart being through his stomach has merit.

Right behind the food came people with iced hour-glass carafes of sweet tea. Each one of us got our own. Call me selfish, but I was pleased about that. I grabbed the neck of the carafe and poured into the empty glass by my platter. There was no way most of the guys in that room could appreciate the quality of that sweet tea. I knew immediately that it'd been made in the sun with real sugar because that's exactly the way my mama does it.

Yes. I know that one glass of tea exceeded recommended sugar doses for a month, but what can I say? I agree with recent science. It *is* an addictive drug. Every southerner knows that. But it's still legal.

Looking at the meal in front of me, I had my doubts that it wasn't planned with me in mind. 'Cause damn. Ambrosia couldn't be better.

With the wait staff in retreat and everybody chowing down, Kellan got to his feet again. "I was saying that we have a few activity options available during the day tomorrow. First is canoeing on the Blanco River. If you're signed up, a van will pick you up tomorrow morning around nine. The spot where we'll put in is about five and a half miles west. You don't have to be experienced and everything you need will be provided. The entire trip including a stop for lunch and the ride back to your hotel is about six hours, which means you'll have time for what they call a 'toes up' around here. I highly recommend taking advantage of the sunscreen offered if you want to be comfortable and look like yourself at the big event tomorrow night.

"You'll be floating downstream so not much paddling will be required, but if you're not used to it, you may hear from your arm muscles when it's over. It's fun though and seeing things from the river is a whole different perspective.

"Second, if we have tennis players, Stefan will organize a match. Transportation, lunch and anything else you need, including shoes and racquets, will be provided. If we have a small group, we'll play at the high school here. If there are more, we'll run down to New Braunfels and play at the John Newcombe Tennis Ranch.

"Third, we have a tour going to San Antonio to see the Alamo and the Riverwalk. It's about an hour's drive each way. A bus has been reserved, but it's more likely the trip will be by minivan."

The winners, most of them, laughed and exchanged looks so there was no doubt that was an inside joke.

"Fourth, horseback riding in the hill country. Again, you do not need experience. You could put your grandmothers on these horses. They're as safe as rocking chairs. However, a word of caution; if you're not accustomed to riding, you will be sore where your ass meets the saddle.

"Fifth, if you're into geology, we can get you a VIP pass to the Canyon Lake Gorge. It's a new geological find that opened up suddenly in 2002 when the lake overflowed. Has dinosaur prints and some pretty incredible rock formations. Anyway the policy is researchers only, but we can get you past the guards if you want to go.

"Last, if you'd rather just lounge around and socialize

with other contestants, this area has been reserved for you through the day tomorrow. You can come here for food, drinks, free wifi, and just hang out. It's not necessary to sign up for lounging.

"Be sure to save room for dessert because they're serving fried fruit pies. Yes. You can eat them with your hands." Kellan picked up a piece of paper and read. "Also Texas chocolate pecan pie, rum pound cake, and blueberry cobbler."

Save room? Did he see the size of the platters they brought us?

I had just shoved a spoonful of Southern potato salad into my mouth and was wondering if I could get dessert to go when Ivan said, "So what are you going to do tomorrow?"

Truthfully, I'd been so caught up in the food, I hadn't given it much thought.

"Don't know," I said. "Either just hang out here or do the canoe thing."

Ivan looked aghast. "Well you can't just hang out here!"

"Why not?"

"Because you'd be missing out on an experience! That's why not. You only get so many chances in life to do *real* things. When you're old, what are you going to say? I hung out in a tent with free wifi?"

"By real things you mean things that aren't electronic?"

He pursed his lips and frowned. "I guess that is what I mean."

"Ivan. You get those chances every day. You may not be offered a canoe trip on a river, but you can look up from your phone or walk out on the street whenever you have the desire, or willpower, as the case may be."

"That's not the same thing." He almost pouted. Oddly, it was appalling and appealing at the same time.

I smiled after taking a big bite of cornbread. "Okay."

"Well, it's not."

"I'm not arguing."

"You have that look."

"Ivan, you don't know me well enough to know my 'looks'." I turned in my chair and looked at him straight on. "Are you gay? Because the competition…"

"No! I'm just saying that hanging back in a tent is a chickenshit approach to life."

Finally. He managed to say something that made sense.

"Yeah. You know what? You're right. I guess I'm going canoeing for the first time tomorrow."

"Really?" He brightened. " 'Cause that's what *I'm* doing."

I chuckled under my breath. "Well, it's a small world."

The ringing of a spoon against a glass brought my attention back to the dais. "I hope you all enjoyed dinner. If we don't see you again until tomorrow night, good luck. Maybe next year you'll be occupying one of these chairs. Signups for activities at the tables they've just set up outside."

When that seemed to be the end, everybody clapped. A few people bolted up from their seats like they were afraid their activity would be full if they didn't stampede the exit.

Ivan stood up. "Aren't you coming?"

"Hell, no," I said. "I'm waiting for dessert."

"Dessert! You couldn't possibly eat anything else without delivering the grand puke of all time."

"I'm getting it to go."

"Okay. I'll sign you up for canoe."

"Thanks, Ivan. That'd be great."

Looking around the room I saw that about ten of us had lingered due to the tantalizing promise of fried pies, chocolate, pecans, and cobbler.

When the waiter, who happened to be a trim fortyish woman, stopped in front of me with a tray of desserts, I said, "Wow. It looks as good as it sounded. Can I get it to go?"

She smiled. "Of course, sir. What would you like?"

"What kinds of fried pies do you have?"

"Apple, peach, and cherry."

"I'll have one peach pie, a slice of chocolate pecan, and just a dab of cobbler just to sample the experience."

Her smile told me that she was having fun with my order. I guessed that not many contestants asked for some of everything to go after eating for three. Or four.

"Five minutes, sir."

"Take your time."

The past winners were lingering around the dais chatting as amiably as if they were fraternity brothers. There was probably nothing remarkable about that. Not only did they live in a small town, but they had witches in common. What was remarkable was that I felt a twinge of envy.

I've never been a grouper. No. I don't mean the fish. I mean the sort of person who joins groups, needs groups, and feels happiest when they're in the middle of a group. In fact it was the first time I ever recall thinking that there might be something for me in the easy camaraderie I was witnessing.

A body appeared in front of me, blocking my view, but offering a white paper sack with handles. When I looked inside, I was stunned to see that they'd included a cloth napkin and stainless flatware.

"Will that do, sir?"

I looked up and smiled. "This has to be the only to-go service in the world that doesn't send you home with paper napkins and plastic sporks."

She nodded and walked away at a things-to-do pace.

I ambled outside to see how the activity signup was progressing.

"Willem."

I stopped when I heard a voice call my name from a few feet behind me. It was Kellan.

"I hope you forgive me for pretending to be a contestant earlier. Just like you guys come to get information from us, we get to take a look at the new crop of hopefuls."

Shaking my head, I said, "Nothing to forgive. Now if I'd said something that had disqualified me, that would be different."

He smiled in his congenial way. "It's tough to read actors. You seem like an okay guy, but you could be acting."

I laughed at that. "Just to ease your mind, I never

landed a single acting job. Not in ten years. If I was any good at it, I wouldn't be here."

"Oh?" His chin angled to the side. "How did you end up here?"

"I was standing in line for the last audition I was ever going to try for. The guy next to me in line handed me a card, said try the witches, and the rest is history."

Holding out his hand, he said, "That's a new one. I'm a collector of stories. Yours is unique."

I shook his hand. "Happy to oblige."

A look of curiosity crossed his face. "You from Texas?"

I shook my head. "Alabama."

He grinned. "What are you doing tomorrow?"

"Canoe."

"Good choice. Popular choice. Raider's in charge." He leaned in close and lowered his voice. "Watch out for him. He thinks turning other people's canoes over is hysterical."

"Wow. Thanks for the tip."

Kellan gave me a manly slap on the shoulder and walked off.

I didn't see Roger or Ivan or any of the others I'd met at the bar or Orientation. There was still a line at one of the tables. I stopped one guy leaving.

"Which activity is that for?"

"The canoe thing. It's the most popular." He looked back at the line. "By far."

chapter four

I HAD JUST finished off the pecan pie and lay back on the bed to watch TV and rub my stomach like a happy Buddha statue, when I heard a knock at the door. I took the precaution of looking through the peephole even though I felt as safe as if I was still in my mother's womb.

Looking up and down the hall, I could see that some-one had left their delivery and disappeared. There was a bundle wrapped in brown paper and tied with corn shuck twine. There was also a card with my name on it.

I closed the door, locked it, placed the package on the bed and unwrapped it like a Christmas present. I never would have guessed what it was in a hundred years. A black long-sleeve, wick-away moisture shirt in my size, dry-on-the-fly camouflage cargo short pants that came to the knee in my size, and black pull on water booties, also in my size.

At that point I should not have been amazed that they knew so much about me or that they were prepared to produce precisely what I needed when I needed it.

"Hmmm," I said to the room, as if that covered it.

So I went to sleep and dreamed of beautiful witches dressed like "I Dream of Jeannie", moving in and out of a white tent where I lay on Persian rugs with tons of pillows, smoking something from a pipe. Each was carrying a platter of constantly changing delectable delicacies and encouraging me to try more. It was a perpetually moving line that seemed to have no end.

I had set the alarm for eight just to be sure that I had time to shave and look halfway awake. Maybe get a coffee in the lobby downstairs.

The clothes and booties fit perfectly and, if you ask me, didn't look too bad on me either. I stuck my phone, wallet, and room key in one of the cargo pockets, zipped it up, and headed down. It was eight fifty and would have been excruciatingly early if I was on my old L.A. lifestyle schedule. But I wasn't. I was a new man in hungry pursuit of Plan B and that was noteworthy for two reasons. First, I had no Plan C. And, second, I didn't really know what Plan B was. I just knew it was focused on the concept of heart's desire. And what could go wrong with that? Right?

The Charmed Horse Hotel had a coffee bar open in the mornings with a barista who could challenge any espresso artiste anywhere in the world. Yes. That includes Italy. I haven't been to Italy, but I feel certain enough to make that claim.

I took my steaming cup of pseudo self-actualization out onto the porch to wait for the van. There were seventeen other guys already waiting, wearing clothes that were similar, but not identical.

At least there's that.

In other words, the hotel's entire weekend occupancy was going canoeing on the Blanco River with a mad

Viking who wanted to turn us over in the water. Christ.

They were standing around on the front porch decking trying to look cool while eyeing each other suspiciously. Ivan wasn't there, but I didn't expect to see him since he's staying somewhere else.

At nine on the nose, three white vans pulled up and stopped right in front of us. Each driver came around and slid the side panel door open.

The driver of the van directly in front of me added, "Watch your step, gentlemen," and smiled.

"Is anybody sitting up front?" I asked.

He looked surprised. "No. You're welcome to shotgun if you want it."

"I do. Better view."

He grabbed the handle of the passenger door and opened it for me. I noticed the other guys giving me dirty looks for being impertinent enough to score a better seat, but I shrugged it off. I wasn't there to make friends and, hey, they could have asked just as easily as I did.

When we pulled away, I said to the driver, "I'm Willem."

He slanted his eyes sideways like he had a secret. "I know who you are Mr. Draiocht."

"I can't say the same. What's your name?"

"Lawson."

"That's a great name. Strong. Unusual."

"Belonged to my granddad."

"Was he from around here?"

"Yep. He was born here, but in case you're wonderin', we're still considered newcomers."

"So how long's the ride?"

" 'Bout eight minutes."

"You going out on the river today?"

He shook his head. "No. I'm going to be waiting for you downstream at the end of the day and drive you back here."

"That's good to know. So what do you do when you're not driving contestants around?"

"Oh. This and that."

"Uh-huh." A snort from behind told me that some-body thought it was funny that I just hit a conversational wall. The rest of the contestants in the van seemed to be listening to us instead of talking amongst themselves. "Have you ever done the canoe thing on the river?"

"Oh, sure. Lots of times."

"Must be fun then."

"Hmmm. If you're a certain kind of person."

I didn't know where to take the conversation from there so I let it drop. We rode the rest of the way in silence, but that was just another couple of minutes.

We pulled off the highway and drove down a dirt road, banked with brush on both sides, for a hundred yards. The dense foliage opened to a grassy riverbank shaded by huge cypress trees.

When Lawson stopped the van, he looked over his shoulder at the other passengers and said, "Grab some breakfast at that truck over there and then get a life jacket. You've got about fifteen minutes before you'll be on the water with a paddle in your hands. Nobody gets on a canoe without a life jacket."

The green bank was littered with brightly painted canoes that looked way too cheerful for a group of guys trying to prove they would never emote because it's not cool.

"Hey! Willem." I heard a shout and turned to see Ivan stuffing something that looked like a tortilla and scrambled eggs into his mouth. I started walking his direction as he was heading in mine. "You've got to try this, man. These people know how to eat."

I checked in with my stomach. It replied that it was still working on last night. So I said, "Looks good, but I ate."

He smiled around a mouthful of breakfast burrito. "So you're gonna share a canoe with me, right?"

He was too teasable for me to let that go. "I don't know, man. Do you have experience?"

Ivan looked crestfallen. He stopped chewing and said, "They said we don't need experience."

I didn't have the heart to play him any longer. "I'm just messin' with you. Of course we're gonna share a boat."

His good-natured demeanor returned immediately. "We're supposed to put on one of those life preservers."

I didn't want to wear one of the bulky, hot life preservers, and knew I didn't need one, but I figured it was a pick-your-battles moment. So I let it go.

One of the helpers stepped up to us. They were easily identified by their khaki shorts and forest green tees.

"Morning, gentlemen," said the kid waving two plastic pouches. "These are for your valuables. Put your phones, wallets, watches, or anything else that can't get wet in here.

These are watertight so long as you seal them up. Put them in one of your big zipper pockets. Buttons come open sometimes, but zippers get even harder to open when they get wet. So you won't lose your stuff no matter what."

I wondered what he meant by 'no matter what', but figured it had something to do with accidentally going in the water.

Ivan and I reached at the same time and followed his instructions while he looked on to make sure we got it right. "Excellent," he enthused. "It's a glorious day for a float down the river."

You have to give it up for somebody who's enjoying his job. At that he moved on to the next group of guys and repeated the instructions.

"So. Let's pick one out," I said.

"Yeah. We don't want to get stuck with yellow or orange."

I had to laugh. "Why? What's wrong with yellow and orange?"

"Oh, don't get me wrong, they're cheerful, but too girlie."

"Alright. How do you rate canoe colors for manliness, Ivan?"

"Well," he said, "nobody can argue with ocean blue. It's universally understood as a boy color."

"Universally," I repeated drily.

"Red is a good strong masculine color. It says, 'If you're lookin' for trouble, you came to the right place'." I laughed, because I couldn't imagine anybody thinking Ivan was trouble. "What?" he said.

"Nothing," I chuckled. "Go on. This is entertaining."

"The green is also a good solid masculine color. It says 'close to nature and the great outdoors' without any hint of feminine compromise."

"Looks like that brings us to orange and yellow."

"Orange and yellow are for pussies."

"Well, then, red, blue, or green it is. Take your pick while you still can."

He opened his mouth, but was stopped by the sound of Raider's bellow. A bunch of the kids in khaki shorts and green tees jumped in the water.

"Line up over here." He pointed to where the grassy bank met a short dock. "We'll get you in the boats in order."

Leaning toward Ivan, I whispered, "So much for color preference." Ivan made a face. "Don't be glum, chum. You know in your heart it doesn't make any difference."

"Yeah." He produced a small smile. "I guess."

We got in line behind about ten other guys. The camp shirt kids on the bank pushed the canoes in. The kids in the river took control, guiding them alongside the dock as they waded through the water.

They held the first canoe still while the first two guys got in and took their seats. They picked up the paddles.

"If you've never done this before," Raider yelled, "don't worry. It's not hard. If you want to turn left, you both paddle on the right side. If you want to go straight, one of you paddles on the right while the other paddles on the left. If there's a big difference in strength, you'll have to make an adjustment, but you'll figure it out. If you lose an paddle, one of you will have to jump in and get it. So try not to lose an paddle.

"After you're in your canoe, paddle out to the middle and wait."

The process was efficient so getting the guys into the canoes didn't take as long as you might expect. There were twelve canoes altogether, plus Raider. So I guess that's thirteen. He stepped into his custom camo green canoe like he'd done it a thousand times, and shoved away. I was a little envious about the fact that he wasn't wearing a stupid life preserver, but whatever. Not my show.

As it turned out we got a yellow canoe, but Ivan seemed to forget all about that as soon as he experienced the sensation of floating on the green water current. He was in front, which was okay with me. I've always had a back-to-the-wall preference.

Ivan and I ended up being in the middle of the cluster, but it didn't feel crowded because everybody just naturally spread out once we were underway. A couple of times Raider rested his paddle and pointed out wildlife, most notably a large buck almost obscured by the trees.

It was peaceful. It was calm. It was serene and, by the time we stopped for lunch, I was so relaxed I felt like a wet noodle. The kids from upstream had motored their way to the lunch stop and were on hand to make sure everybody got out of their canoes without mishap.

Catering had been set up in a shady clearing where they'd been grilling shish-ka-bob over charcoal. There were choices of chicken and peppers, veggie only, beef teriyaki with squash and onions. Whole corn on the cob, also on sticks, and plenty of everything for seconds, thirds, or fourths.

I saw the wisdom of choosing food that could be eaten on a stick.

They offered an iced-down choice of water, vitamin water, and a few soft drinks.

This was topped off by fried pies. You may find it unbelievable, but I declined. I didn't want to fart my way through the big event that night.

A short forty-five minutes later we were back in the water and headed downstream again. When we were, by my estimation, an hour or so from our destination, I saw Raider begin to drop back. He paddled lazily, letting the other canoes go by. As we passed he said, "Are you enjoying yourself, Mr. Draiocht?"

"It's been a good day," I responded.

"It's too deep to wade here. You know that?"

Just then I caught a glint in Raider's eye. I don't know how I knew it, but I had the uncanny sense the fucker was going to try to turn *my* canoe over.

Maybe I went temporarily crazy, but I was just as sure that I didn't want to sit by and let that happen.

So I said, "If I lived here, I'd do this a lot." I was smiling all the while he was coming closer, pulling up alongside. Just when I judged that I had the perfect angle, I stuck the tip of my paddle under the keel of his canoe and using the side of my canoe for leverage, pushed down with all my might.

Yep. You guessed it. The canoe turned over and a very surprised-looking Raider went under. Seconds later an even more surprised-looking Raider popped back up flailing.

"I can't swim," he shouted. "I don't have a life vest and I can't fucking swim!"

Shit. I hadn't considered that as a possibility. I unzipped my life preserver as I jumped over the side. When I reached him, I knew I was going to have a fight on my hands trying to get the life vest on him because he was panicking.

Sure enough. He grabbed onto me, dunked me and held me under with his considerable bulk until my lungs were ready to burst. Suddenly he let go and I felt a big paw grab my shirt and pull me to the surface. I dragged in a ragged breath like I'd been drowning, which I suppose I was. When my air passages began to relax, I looked at Raider, who was treading water and laughing.

"It's nice to know you'd jump in for me if I was drownin'." I probably looked at him like he was crazy because that's exactly what I was thinking. He lowered his voice, "Who told you somebody always gets dunked?"

"Don't know what you're talking about, liar," I spat. I must have gone insane to be calling Raider names, but I was pissed. I tried to save his ass and he thanked me for it by trying to kill me.

His head went back and he guffawed. "Good one, little brother. You're the only one to ever get me first. It could be real entertainin' to have you around."

I swam over to the canoe where Ivan was looking distraught.

"Put all your weight into leaning away from me when

I say go," I told him.

Ivan performed like a pro, which allowed me to pull myself back into the canoe with as much ease as wet clothes and water drag will allow.

"Smooth," said Raider, still watching, still treading water.

"Go on," he told everybody. "I'll catch up. When you get to the green shirts, stop."

Raider swam to where somebody was holding his canoe steady. Somebody else had fished his paddle out of the river before it disappeared downstream. He took the paddle and guided the canoe to the shallows with his other arm, feet kicking. When he could stand up in waist-deep water, he righted the canoe and pulled himself in.

"Hope you didn't make yourself an enemy," Ivan said.

"Well, his intention was to turn us over. This way, only I got wet."

Ivan looked over his shoulder with a grin and laughed. "In that case, thank you, 'brother'." Ivan smirked at the term Raider had used.

Chapter Five

After my dunking and subsequent near drowning, I needed a nap. Or a 'toes up' as they reportedly say in Wimberley. I was careful to set my alarm because naps had been causing near-misses lately. It had been made clear to the contestants that, if we missed our transportation, scheduled to arrive at nine o'clock, we'd be out of luck.

At eight, I enjoyed a long hot shower, gave myself a close shave and the Willem's-best mussed hairdo.

Why wouldn't they just say what they wanted us to wear? Lot less stress.

Maybe that was the point. Maybe they wanted us to feel off our game. I wished I had rented black tie before I'd left L.A. It's always better to be *over*dressed. Right?

Too late to worry about that. So I got out my black jeans, my black zipper ankle boots, and a red raw silk shirt with extra pointed collar. I hadn't planned to wear that, just threw it in at the last minute. I pulled the ironing board out of the closet and pressed it in the room. I thought it draped my body in a way that accentuated the width of my shoulders and the vee of my waist, so I left the tail out.

They kept saying that the right person couldn't do the wrong thing, or something like that. So taking them at their word, I took one last look in the mirror and left for the ultimate contest.

There were a handful of guys waiting for the elevator as I passed it by. I saw that they'd opted for dark suits or tuxes. Couldn't fault them for that. If I'd given it more thought, I'd have done the same.

I nodded and kept going. I figured the hotel had a grand staircase that went all the way to the top floor because somebody thought it would be used.

Stepping out onto the hotel porch, I saw more suits. There was no point fretting over it, as my grandmother would say.

Right on time, three black stretch limos pulled up in a line just as it was getting dark. Easy math. Eighteen rooms in the hotel. Eighteen contestants, six to a car. I decided to try the shotgun trick again. I walked up to the driver of the first vehicle.

"Hey, I'm Willem," I said.

"Yes. Good evening, Mr. Draiocht."

"I was wondering if anyone's claimed the passenger seat in front."

His jaw went slack from surprise, but he recovered quickly and chuckled. "No one has, Mr. Draiocht. Would you like to sit up front?"

"Love to. I didn't get your name."

"Anselm, sir," he said as he opened the passenger door for me.

I settled in feeling like I'd scored a coup. While the

other guys would be riding sideways on bench seats, giving each other the stink eye, I'd be looking forward like God intended, seeing where I was going, just the way I liked it.

When we pulled away, I said, "How long have you been driving, Anselm?"

"You mean how long have I had a chauffeur license? 'Bout six years."

"Do you work out of Austin or San Antonio?"

"Nope. Wimberley."

I looked at him with open disbelief. "From what I've seen of Wimberley, I'd be surprised that the locals could keep you busy."

He smiled and gave me a sideways glance. "Busy enough. Sometimes I take jobs elsewhere."

We began our ascent, winding up through the hills that mirrored what we'd seen at the Orientation, palatial villas dotting the hillscape like gems. Within five minutes we pulled up to a guardhouse at a massive outer iron gate. When Anselm lowered the window and showed himself, the guard opened the gate. We drove inside about twenty feet and waited while the gate closed behind us. When it was secure the inner gate opened and we drove forward.

I looked behind us. "Are the other two cars going through that same process?"

Anselm looked amused. "You've got a lot of questions for somebody who hasn't won yet, Mr. Draíocht. You just concentrate on gettin' yourself a witch. Tonight that should be the only thing on your mind."

Should it? I still wasn't sure what I was even doing in a limo in Wimberley, Texas, having just passed through a security setup that would do the mafia proud.

The climb quickly went from a gentle slope to steep ascent.

"Wow. Great for skateboarding."

Anselm chuckled. "I hear some of the young ladies use the incline for just that purpose. Personally I don't get it. Beating yourself up like that?" He shook his head.

We turned into a lane lined with trees on both sides that gave no clue as to where we might be headed, but within a minute it opened onto an estate that would put most of Beverley Hills to shame. There were tiers of gardens, each with room for car parking tastefully worked into the design. It was unique, charming, and practical.

The house looked like a grand English manor with gas light sconces every few feet. The design was centuries old, but the house was flawlessly new.

"Here you are, sir," said Anselm. "If you wait, I'll come 'round and open the door for you."

I grinned. "No need. Thanks for the ride."

"Anytime." He smiled and touched the bill of his chauffeur's cap.

I could hear music coming from the house as soon as I opened the car door. Suited young men were spilling out of limousines and heading toward the open door. I filed in behind them, feeling a rush of excitement to finally learn why I'd let myself get caught up in this mysterious pursuit of the last thing I wanted, a wife. I was too curious to withdraw from the competition once I found out what it was about. Certainly I'm not the marrying sort. I've known that about myself since I was a child.

Some of the winners were in the foyer greeting contestants as we arrived. There was a large living room to the left, where the music was coming from. I craned my neck around a couple of fellow contestants and saw that it was a lone musician with two keyboards, a mic, and a guitar sitting off to the side. It was very impressive. He was managing to make a lot of decent-sounding music for a solo act, kind of a pop/new age fusion.

I noticed Kellan, but that wasn't surprising. He's the sort of guy who gets noticed by women *and* men. I'll bet that, if he'd tried acting, he would have gotten every role he went for. That aside and, more to the point, he was wearing a linen sports coat open over a concert tee, with jeans and runners. As I passed by him, he caught my eye and said, "Lots of food. Lots of drink. Feel free to wander around, but be sure to spend time in the ballroom so you can mingle. You can't win if you don't play."

He smiled as if that held some deep and secret meaning and was not just the everyday expression people use to describe why they buy lottery tickets. It also felt like it was being said for me alone, but I quickly shook that thought away and chalked it up to imagination. I wasn't special. Just another guy in the cattle call line waiting to be auditioned for a part I wasn't sure I wanted.

Life is strange.

I fell in with the flow of the crowd. The first room I passed on my right had a few benches and chairs around the walls, but the feature was a mountain of oysters on the half shell on ice. It was such a ridiculous display of wealth it was almost obscene. Standing at the doorway staring probably made me look like the guy who'd never been to the city, but it was amazing by anybody's standards.

A big paw landed on my shoulder hard.

"Hey, hero." I turned and found myself at eye level with Raider's larynx. I had to tilt my head back to see his face. Nodding at the oysters, he said, "Flown in from Alaska this morning. This month may not end in an R, but these babies are goo-ood."

I looked at the oysters again. "They look good."

"Yeah," he said. "They are. Just like life here."

Raider was wearing a black Henley, olive-colored cargo pants and black biker boots. At least one guy was *more* casual than I was.

"Looks like," I agreed.

"You know the way to the ballroom?"

"Uh, no."

"Come on. I'll take you. Least I can do for the guy who tried to save my life." He laughed at that and slapped me on the shoulder again, hard enough that I almost lost my footing.

Thinking that saying no to Raider was a bad idea, I let him show me to the ballroom. We passed a few more rooms with mega food displays, each display of opulence trying to outdo the one before. It was clear they wanted to impress somebody.

Raider turned to the left down a hallway that appeared to be taking us to a different wing. The music from the entrance had faded away and I was beginning to hear strains of medieval wind and wire coming from ahead. Apparently it called to my subconscious because I realized

I'd quickened my steps as we approached.

We passed windows that looked out onto an immense greenhouse built on a tier a few feet lower than the main house.

"That's where they grow herbs and, you know, stuff. Some flowers, too. You know," Raider said.

No. Not sure that I did know anything except that I didn't want to argue with Raider.

"That's nice."

He chuckled. "So. Not into horticulture, I guess. Me neither."

We were nearing a pair of big double doors, six feet wide, eight feet high. As we approached they swung inward in front of us as if they were feather light, like magic. But that magic couldn't begin to compare with what was inside.

Three dozen crystal chandeliers lit the rectangular room, which actually formed a separate wing of the house. The forty-foot ceiling was covered in murals of mythological creatures most of which I could identify. Broad terraces, romantically lit by gas lights, were built on both sides of the room, with a series of French doors. Since the night was nice, the doors had been left open so that guests could come and go.

Wait staff moved smoothly between conversational clusters offering various drinks and all manner of hors d'oeuvres from light to heavy, common to exotic.

The music was even more compelling inside the ballroom. A four-piece ensemble, wearing medieval costume, were playing dulcimer, flute, Celtic harp, and fiddle. I thought I'd never heard anything so enchanting.

It's hard to explain how I was able to take all this in and process it well enough to tell you what I saw, because nothing I've described could begin to compare with, what I assumed were, the witches.

There were about twenty, each wearing a cocktail dress the same value of red as my shirt. People in L.A. like to tell themselves constantly that no other city has so many beautiful women. All I can say is that those fools have never been to a Witches' Ball in Wimberley.

"So, you're one of us!" said a bright voice from behind me.

I turned to see a woman with mahogany hair and deep blue eyes. Her lipstick was the same color as her dress and only one description fitted her. Stunning.

"Excuse me?"

She nodded at my chest. "Your shirt. You seemed to know the exact right thing to wear."

I looked down at my shirt stupidly as if I'd forgotten what I was wearing. "I was actually worried about the choice until just now. Thank you for the reassurance."

She laughed. "You shouldn't need reassurance, Willem. You're all that. Don't you know? I'm Harmony."

"Hi. I'm… well, I guess you already know…" I trailed off.

She laughed again. "Don't be nervous, Willem. You have no reason to be."

She took my arm in hers and began walking toward the center of the room. I had no choice but to let her guide me. Well, I suppose that's not true. I could have jerked away and said, "Keep your hands to yourself, bitch", but going along seemed like a much better idea. And besides I was curious as to what was going to happen next.

"Are you one of the, um, prizes?"

She smiled up at me. "We're not supposed to say. Only those of us who are close to debutante age attend these events. It works on two levels. The contestants don't know who's coming out and there are enough of us to form a quorum."

"A quorum?"

"A body of sufficient number to make a decision for the extended group."

"So any of the lovely ladies might be…"

She nodded. "So you met my little sister."

"Destiny? She's your sister?"

"Yeah." Harmony chuckled. "You made an impression."

"I made an impression?!? Whatever my impression was, it doesn't come close to the illusion she cast. I thought I saw a black bear vanish from the middle of the street and reappear on the hotel porch as a shame-faced Beagle."

Harmony shook her beautiful head. "So you met Izzy, too. She didn't tell me that. He has a bear fantasy."

"She said that."

"And it wasn't an illusion. If you win, you're going to have to get used to seeing reality from a different perspective."

I stopped. "How different?"

"You like your life right now?"

"That's kind of personal."

"It's a personal night. Answer."

"No."

"Do you want to like your life?"

"That's a stu… I mean, of course. Everybody wants to like their lives."

She turned and faced me. "No, Willem. Everyone doesn't. Lots of people are satisfied with the misery they know."

I wished I could say I had no idea what she was talking about, but the truth was that I knew exactly what she meant.

"People can change." I stopped, having just added two and two. "Destiny said her sister was coming out tonight. Since you're her sister, does that mean that…?"

"No, but nice try. It's another sister."

"Oh." I'm sure I looked disappointed. "Does she look like you?"

She grinned, ignoring my question. "Now here's what you're going to do." She patted my captive arm with her free hand. "Mingle. Chat with all the women. At midnight, the two who have summoned husbands will announce their choices and the ceremony will be tomorrow."

"Ring the bell, snuff out the candle?"

Her blue eyes opened wide. She was surprised, but she didn't seem angry. "That is part of the ceremony. How did you…?"

"Harmony. Who have we here?" One of the other witches was standing close and demanding to be introduced.

"Lyra, this is Willem."

"Oh, yes. Willem. Are you having fun?"

"I, ah, yes. I just got here."

"Have you had something to eat? We wouldn't want you to be hungry and there's *so* much food!"

"I'll never forget the food."

She barked out a laugh. "You hope!"

It took me a second to catch up and remember about the memory wipe thing.

"Well, yeah, I guess I do hope I remember. You could hide a body under the oysters."

Her grin resolved into a smile. "So tell me what you're going to do with your life if you win, Willem."

"You know, that still sounds like one of those what-would-you-do-if-you-got-a-million-dollars questions. It feels too unreal to take seriously."

She nodded. "A good solid honest answer. I like that." After studying me for a few seconds, she said, "Okay. You passed my test. Let me introduce you to Lilith."

She turned me around when she took my arm and, as she did, I happened to catch a heated look exchanged between Harmony and Raider. It was an, "Ah ha," moment immediately followed by an, "Oh, crap," moment when I realized that, if I won Harmony's sister, Raider would be my brother-in-law. I understood why he was happy enough to star in the Orientation video and babysit inexperienced canoers on the river. She was a catch and he knew it.

I decided there were worse things than being in Raider's family. He didn't actually *finish* drowning me in the river, but at the time it felt like he was trying. On the other hand, he insisted on showing me to the ballroom. And he called me 'hero'.

Who couldn't get used to that?

I was ushered from one beautiful woman to the next and each took measure of me in her own way. It was an interview, or audition, but it was the most pleasant I'd ever experienced. Or ever would, I was sure.

Still, after an hour or so, I was getting hungry. When Bless tried to walk me to another chat, I balked.

"Hey, could you maybe give me a couple of minutes to partake of some of the amazing feast stations? I haven't eaten and that guy in the other part of the house carving that prime rib really spoke to me."

Bless had a laugh that didn't exactly sound like tinkling bells, but reminded me of them just the same. "Certainly, Willem. Would you like me to accompany you?"

"That would be..." I happened to look away and notice that most of the conversational groups in the room consisted of clusters of contestants, not a witch in sight. I realized that was what I'd been seeing the whole time whenever I looked away from the woman I was talking with. "Bless, I hope this isn't an inappropriate question, but am I getting special treatment?"

She treated me to an extra big helping of her tinkling bells laugh. "Willem, you're quite perceptive. And you've passed my test."

"You know, you're the sixth or seventh person to say that to me. Is this a gauntlet of gorgeous women in sexy red dresses?"

Again the laugh. "I love that description. You're quite a character, Willem. You would fit in around here." As she smiled at me, she grabbed the elbow of another beauty passing by. "Glory, this is Willem."

When Glory smiled, I knew how she came by her name. "Hi, Willem."

"He's hungry and headed in the direction of prime rib."

"Of course he is. I don't see a man like this eating watercress."

"Yes, well, perhaps you'd like to accompany him while he dines."

Glory seemed as ecstatic as if she'd won the prize herself. "Of course! Willem. I'd be honored."

She slipped her arm in mine and walked me to the prime rib. "What would you like with that?" she asked. "While Raleigh is slicing your rib just the way you want it, I'll gather up something to go with it."

"You sure?"

"Yes. Idle hands are the devil's workshop, you know."

"Okay, then. Caesar salad. And did I see au gratin potatoes?" She nodded. "That should do."

She pointed to a table at the rear of the room. "I'll meet you right there."

She was there with salad and spuds before I arrived with a hunk of prime rib that smelled so good it was all I could do to not face plant into the plate and tear into it with my teeth. The promise of Bearnaise sauce on the side helped me keep it together so that I managed to preserve enough dignity to sit and take a few bites of salad before digging into my current reason for living with fork and knife.

Out of nowhere a waiter appeared on my right pouring red wine into my glass. That was followed by a delivery of ice water seconds later.

"You've eaten?" I asked Glory, who sat smiling with her legs crossed as if there was nothing in the universe she'd rather be doing than watching me eat.

"Much earlier."

Someone appeared with a mint garnished drink that I hadn't heard Glory order.

"I've decided that Wimberley must have the best service in the world. I'm certain the Queen of England is envious."

She smiled. "She might be. But you know, you get what you pay for, Willem."

"So I've heard. I'm just a middle class boy from Alabama so I wouldn't have much personal experience in that department."

"You don't strike me as someone who thinks of Golden Bull Buffet as a special occasion."

"I had some nice times courtesy of my agent. Learned the difference between a fruit fork and a soup spoon."

"Your agent? Oh, that's right. You were an actor."

"How is it that everyone seems to know so much about me? Have you memorized bios on all fifty contestants? And come to think of it, why did you say 'were an actor'?"

"First, yes. We look over incoming guests. Second, some of us just learn names, some of us read more and have good recall. Third, you told our people in L.A. that you're done with acting. That puts it in the past tense, right?"

"Right. So, should I be asking questions about you?"

She grinned. "You're funny, Willem."

"Why's that?"

"Because you *have* been asking questions."

Hearing her say it out loud, I realized that was true.

"This prime rib is indescribable. And the wine, he didn't ask me for a preference, but I've gotta tell you. It's amazing."

"If you win, you'll eat whatever you want when you want it. As far as the staff goes, they're very skilled at reading people and anticipating needs."

"Or desires."

"You're quick, Willem. I like that. And you've passed my test. You've made quick work of that rib. Want more?"

I sat back and put both hands on my stomach. "I've eaten more in the past two days than I'd normally eat in a week. No. I'm good."

"Well, maybe coffee and dessert later. I know several people who would be very happy to keep you company when you're ready."

"That's nice."

"Meantime, let's get back to business. We have a few more people to introduce you to."

True to her word, Glory delivered me into the hands of another knockout who then passed me on to someone else. I'd counted how many beautiful creatures I'd talked to over the course of the evening and, if I wasn't woozy from too much alcohol, I was carrying a total of twenty-nine. That meant there was one to go.

I was ushered toward the last inquisitor at twenty minutes before midnight. She had her back to me and was chatting with four contestants. She had long black hair falling in shiny waves down a backless dress that revealed just the right amount of muscle under flawless skin. The dress was a perfect complement to her hourglass figure.

"Ravish, this is Willem."

When she turned around, I felt the hair follicles on my head stand straight up, joining the goosebumps that suddenly popped out all over my body. I know I lost my breath for a minute. It was the woman from the portrait, but in the flesh. She was even wearing the same dress.

Her pale green eyes swept over my face, down my body and back up, just before she smiled with lips the same color as her dress.

"Hello, Willem." Her voice was as sultry as a siren and beckoned me to lean in unconsciously. "Let's go outside on the terrace."

I think that, if she'd said let's jump into a cauldron of boiling oil, I would have taken her hand and agreed. It only took a moment for me to decide that I had to have her, even if it meant killing every other contestant with my bare hands to get rid of the competition.

"Alright," was the best I managed.

As the others had done before her, she slipped her hand through the crook of my elbow, but unlike the others before her, I felt a weird sort of tingly sensation from the contact.

"Are you having a good time?" she asked.

I was a little taller so that she was looking up at me, even with heels on. And I liked that.

"I am. Especially now."

I hadn't realized that probably sounded more cheesy than charming until it rolled out of my mouth without putting any thought behind it, but her smile told me it was an okay thing to say.

"Don't be so worried, Willem. The right person can't say the wrong thing."

"That's, ah, very deep."

"Is it?"

We stopped when we reached the banister that edged the terrace and formed a barrier to walking off the hillside. She turned to face me. The gaslights flickered like torches, making her eyes seem even more hypnotic.

"So, Willem, do you want to win?"

"Being perfectly honest, I'm not entirely sure why I'm here, let alone *what* I might win."

"Me."

"You what?"

"Do you want to win me?"

Every fiber of every cell in my body began jumping up and down and screaming, "Yes! Yes! Yes!" I wasn't sure what winning Ravish entailed, but whatever it meant, I was sure I wanted in. I felt like I truly understood the meaning of the word 'bewitched'.

"Ravish, I..."

"Kiss me, Willem. Then you can decide."

That was an offer I could *not* have refused if I'd wanted to. And I didn't want to.

I put my hands on either side of her hips and pulled her into me, thinking that at any second the crowd was going to spill outside with kazoos and laughter saying, "Gotcha! You didn't really think *you* could win. Did you?" But as she drew closer nothing happened.

I brushed her lips with mine lightly. Once. Twice. Then allowed my mouth to settle on the sweet soft fullness of hers. I knew I was going to look ridiculous in red lipstick, but I didn't care. That kiss wasn't just a kiss. It was more spectacular than most orgasms.

At the point where I would normally ease up for a breath, I pulled her in tighter, unwilling to let go of what might be the peak experience of my entire life. Eventually my lungs had their way. I pulled back and looked at her. That's when I saw it. She was looking at me as if *she* was the one who'd won the prize.

Holy crap! I was going to be a winner.

"Willem, you probably don't know it yet, but you were made for me. And you're going to be a winner if you accept the contract I'll offer you tonight."

Only one cylinder of my brain was firing, but I still managed to put it together.

"You're Destiny's sister."

She grinned. "Yes."

"And your other sister is married to Raider."

She looked surprised. "Yes. How did you know?"

"I caught them giving each other a look. The important thing is that I accept."

"Well," she smiled, "you can't accept without going

over the terms, but we'll only be offering two contracts this year and yours is one of them. We should go back inside. It's almost midnight."

All of a sudden I was feeling self-conscious about the crowd, especially Raider and Kellan. "I have red lipstick all over."

She laughed. It was the exact opposite of a tinkling bells laugh. It was the laugh of a bawdy bar maid who'd seen and done it all. I *loved* it. So did my cock, that couldn't seem to stop trying to twitch its way out of my pants.

"There's no lipstick to come off, Willem. My lips are this color."

"You look like this twenty-four hours a day?"

I didn't care if I was being pranked at that point. I held my arm out for her and she took it in her sexy, but elegant way.

"Maybe not, but my mouth doesn't change. Have I told you that you look delicious in this color?" she asked, but I didn't have a chance to answer because we walked through the door to a cheer from the women and the past winners.

Harmony came to greet us. "Ladies and gentlemen. Two of our guests will be offered contracts this year. Willem Draiocht by Ravish Wimberley. And Cairn Connelly by Deli Bennett. To all the rest of you, thank you for coming. As you return to your homes you will lose all memory of what you've seen and heard here. You will have pleasant memories of your visit to Wimberley, but will not associate it with any purpose beyond leisure.

Good night."

I could see the other contestants smirking at each other like they didn't believe for a minute they'd forget a second of their experience.

Harper and Ivan were the only two who made a point to come by and congratulate me.

Looking at Ravish, Ivan said, "You're a lucky man, Will. She's something."

I looked at Ravish feeling like I was having an out of body experience. "She is."

"You can enter again, Ivan," she said. "And you should. Perhaps your contract just wasn't ready for you yet."

He smiled. "I'll bet you say that to all the contestants."

"I assure you that I do not. I mean it sincerely."

"We'll see. Thanks for the encouragement."

"That was nice of you," I said, looking down at my prize.

"Not at all. It's true. He may be a future winner."

"So you really know who the winners are before we arrive?"

She nodded, smiling. "Yes. The others are just here to make the winners feel comfortable. That and males like competition."

I laughed. "That's why the ruse? Males like competition?"

"It works." She shrugged. "Haven't you felt at ease this weekend?"

I thought back. "Well, yeah. Except when Raider was trying to drown me."

Kellan appeared in front of me with his arm around Glory. "Congratulations, Will. It's a very special brotherhood you're joining."

Glory either squeezed his butt cheek or pinched him. It was hard to tell. But he jumped.

He looked down at her. "You know it's hard to maintain a sense of dignity when you insist on treating me like a male stripper."

She gave him a playful pout. "Sorry, Sugarbunch. I'm working on it."

His answering lopsided grin said he'd tolerate anything she served up.

I looked down to see a large, sleek black cat trying to twirl itself around Glory's legs. She leaned over and picked the cat up, saying, "Hey, Fambo. You need some attention?"

She brought the cat up and held it in her arms. It looked at me with the heavy lids of extreme pleasure partially covering pale green eyes that were eerily similar to the color of Ravish's. Its purring was loud enough to be heard several feet away.

"This is my cat, Willem. He and Kellan both think they're king of this castle. And they're both a little jealous of my attentions to the other." She shifted the cat so that her nose was touching his. "Can't be helped. I need both my bad boys."

I looked at Kellan, who rolled his eyes. He clearly didn't share Glory's affection for the cat. "So this is your house?"

"It is." He raised his chin a bit in an obvious moment

of pride. "Most of the community gatherings and such are held here because we have extra space."

"That's an understatement," I replied.

"Excuse me. I need to talk to Harmony," Glory said.

When she turned to go, cat draped over her shoulder, Kellan said, "Looks like we'll see you back here tomorrow."

"Looks like. Any tips?"

"No." He grinned. "You don't need any tips. You won."

When he walked off, I turned to Ravish. "Has anyone ever told you that you look exactly like Pleasant Wimberley?"

She looked genuinely surprised. "No, Willem. How would you know that?"

"One of the gallery owners told me I'd been pranked, that she shows herself to people in other portraits sometimes. You look exactly like her. She was even wearing this dress."

"This dress?" She looked down. "But these are modern clothes."

"Guess she likes contemporary fashion."

Ravish treated me to her sexy, throaty laugh. "You're a character, Willem."

"That's what people keep telling me."

"And I'm so lucky to be your prize."

The idea of winning seemed about as real to me as unicorns leaping over rainbows, but I guess some people would say that ghosts don't haunt hotels, and long-deceased pioneer women don't temporarily occupy oil-painted portraits in red cocktail dresses. The idea that this heavenly creature might think she was lucky to get me was mind-boggling.

I searched her eyes and shook my head, not knowing what to say. Seemed to me that it was only a matter of time before she changed her mind about being lucky. Sooner or later she'd find out who I really was and feel tragically unfortunate. I'm just a penniless guy who spent ten years chasing a dream that wasn't even mine. That probably defines loser. Further, I was pretty sure I was about to make the world's lousiest groom-for-a-year.

For one thing, I'd never been in the habit of putting somebody else first and I'd heard that's one of the things you do when you want a long term relationship. I shrugged internally, deciding that I was gonna have a hell of a lot of fun before they discovered that I was a fraud.

Harmony winked at me as she handed scrolls to both Ravish and Deli. Yeah. I'm talking about *actual* parchment scrolls, rolled up and sealed with wax. When Ravish broke the seal and began to unroll, I saw that it had been written in hand-inked calligraphy. My fingers itched to touch it almost as badly as they wanted to roam over Ravish's body.

She turned to me. "It's written in Old English language and script. You may not be able to read it."

"No. I can. My hobby has taken me in that direction so it's not new. You want me to read it?"

She held out the scroll and nodded. "It says that you will enter into a trial marriage with me for a year. At the end of a year and a day, which is when the ceremony will take place, you can decide to leave or make it permanent."

I don't know what made me say it because, at the moment, the only thing I wanted was to sign on the dotted line, but something made me say, "I can leave, no hard feelings?"

The way she looked at me made me sorry I'd asked the question. Her smile disappeared and her eyes looked, I don't know, almost plaintive. "Of course," she said, but I could see that I'd planted a seed of worry in her heart. I regretted it, but at the same time, thought perhaps it was for the best.

Just in case.

Because contracts are serious.

I opened the scroll and read through. It was just what she'd said except that there was also a lot of language about the benefits of being a first year groom. And every one of them sounded like a lottery win.

I smiled, hoping to restore her good mood. "Yes. I'm all yours."

It felt strange to say the words, 'I'm yours', to another person. I'd never had a girlfriend for longer than two weeks. My inexperience informed me that I knew nothing about managing the practical or emotional aspects of a long term relationship. But I knew, with Ravish standing next to me in all her delectable perfection, that I'd be an idiot to walk away.

"Where do I sign?"

Ravish pointed to a high table with a bottle of ink. When I got up close I saw that it wasn't a quill pen, but an ink pen decorated with a feather. I picked it up and looked at the bottle. I'd never loaded an ink pen before.

"It's full," she said. "Just take off the cap. You want to go first. Or me?"

"Me."

I signed in my best cursive, glad that I have a decent looking signature, then handed the pen to her.

She signed underneath, never taking her eyes off me. Her signature was just like her. Feminine with a hint of formidable will underneath.

She capped the pen, pressed the front of her body into me, pulled me down so that she could rest her forehead against mine, and said, "Take me home."

"Unless you want to go to a third floor room at the Charmed Horse, that's going to have to be my line."

She laughed softly. "Your things have already been moved to *our* home. Let's go."

"They must have been pretty damn sure I'd say yes."

She laughed while sliding her arm around my waist. My arm went around her shoulders as naturally as if we'd done that a thousand times before. As we walked toward the door, there was some applause behind us, but all that I and my male bits could think about was what was coming next.

As we emerged from the entrance, there was a red Porsche Boxster Spyder sitting right in front of us with the top down.

"You want to drive?" she asked.

"Hell, yes." She started toward the passenger side. "But I haven't driven in a long time. I don't have a car in L.A."

"You didn't forget how, Willem. And it's not far

away."

She smiled and that smile made me feel like I could do anything. So I slid behind the wheel and she handed me the key. I loved that the car had an actual key ignition and not a button start. The fob proudly displayed the colorful Stuttgart stallion emblem and was a work of art in itself.

The engine rumbled to life, purring like it wanted nothing more than to eat up the road.

"Take us home," she said.

Those were three words I never thought I'd hear a woman say to me. I supposed I might get used to it. In time.

At the foot of Kellan's driveway she pointed left. "That way."

We drove around the base of the hill then climbed even higher. She directed me to the last house on the right. I pulled into the circular drive and whistled.

It was a Greek revival with Corinthian columns. On seeing it for the first time, my thought was that it suited her perfectly. Sexy, elegant, and slightly at odds with the Hill Country environment.

"Let's put it in the garage," she said, indicating that I should drive around the house.

The four-car garage was rear entry. She snagged the remote from the driver's side visor and pushed the button so that the door was opening when I made the turn. I pulled in next to a four-wheel drive Jeep.

"You go off-roading?" I asked with an eyebrow raised, trying to picture that.

She lifted a shoulder and looked coy. "Sometimes.

Would you like to walk around and go in the front? Since it's your first time here?"

It seemed like what she wanted, and since I was eager to please, I said, "Sure. You're going to give me the grand tour."

She laughed softly. "If you want."

We walked back around the house to the front door. She didn't use a key, but walked right in. When the front door opened, lamps came on in the entry hall and adjoining rooms.

"You leave your door unlocked?"

"*Our* door," she corrected. "And yes. No one can come in uninvited."

"They can't?"

She laughed again. "No, Willem. What kind of a witch would I be if I couldn't protect my own property from trespassers?"

"Well," I said, "I suppose that's true. About the witch thing..."

"Come in. Let me show you around. Then we can have a drink and talk as long as you like."

I had to admit that talking wasn't my first priority and the idea of a long talk was a little disappointing, but I'd opened the door, so to speak.

The ceilings were sixteen feet high. The décor was simple and livable, but luxurious. Minimalist softened to plush posh. Very Architectural Digest.

I whistled. "Your decorator is really something."

"That would be me." She beamed. "Come on. Let's do a run-through. This is the music room." She pointed to the right. There was a shiny black grand piano shell with a Roland keyboard inside. "I don't play, but Destiny does. It gives her something to do when she visits.

"This is the living room. It pretty much goes unused except for occasional guests." I followed her down the hallway past the staircase that rose from the rear rather than the front of the house. She waved to a room on the right. "That's the study. I don't use it much, but the architect insisted the house wouldn't be complete without it."

I stood staring into the room covered in rich mahogany with its coffered ceiling and built-in shelves and thought, "Yeah. I could see myself there." The room was just about the same size as the entire apartment I shared with Hector and worth more than the entire apartment building. The walls followed the windows as they bowed outward into a semicircle.

"What does the view look like in the daytime?"

"Oh," she said, "you can see the hills, a few of the other houses, the river and part of the town. I think it's nice."

"Sounds like. It's a beautiful room."

"If you want it, it's yours, Willem. You can redecorate it any way you want."

"That's very generous. I might take you up on that. If you're really not using it."

"Willem, you can have anything you want. All you have to do is ask."

That was going to take some getting used to. Whoever thinks they're going to be standing in front of a preposterously gorgeous creature, possibly of supernatural origins, being told you can have anything you want? It occurred to me that I could be dreaming, but everything was just too real, including the smell of Ravish's hair when she passed close by. I don't know scents enough to tell you what she smelled like, just that it was intoxicating.

"You want a drink before we go upstairs?" she asked as she was walking away.

I followed. "Sure. What do you have?"

She laughed. "Everything. *We* have everything."

The kitchen left me almost speechless. The cabinets were painted white, with glass fronts and interior lights. Some of them were so tall that a ladder would have been required. There was a slate island three feet wide and twelve feet long. Above that were a series of lighted pot racks with hanging cookware, copper bottoms gleaming like they'd never been used. One entire wall was dedicated to refrigeration. There was a two-foot-wide wine column, a double freezer column, and a triple refrigerator column.

She pointed to the refrigerator column that had a glass front. "We could open wine if you want, or something stronger. But like I said, we have everything."

True to her word, the glass front column held every kind of soft drink, water, wine cooler, and beer. My eyes ran over the rest of the room. Triple oven. Six burner gas stove.

"Do you live here alone?" I asked.

"Not anymore." She smiled. "Sit." She pointed to one of the leather stools around the island. "Let me get you something. What will you have?"

"What are you having?"

"Hmmm. Coffee?"

I grinned. "Sold."

"How do you take it?"

"I like girlie creamers when I can get them. Otherwise, couple spoons of sugar and milk."

"Girlie creamers?" she asked, as she pulled open one of the other refrigerator columns. "We have every variety of Baileys. Hazelnut. French Vanilla. Original. Crème Brulee. Caramel."

"Stop. That's the one."

"Caramel? Hmmm. I'll have that, too."

She set the Baileys caramel creamer on the bar in front of me and went about brewing the joe in a pod coffeemaker. I remembered that it was days ago when I'd been thinking I wanted to own one of those one day.

She pushed my cup in front of me along with a silver sugar bowl and spoon.

"Fancy."

"The sugar bowl? Is it?"

"Yeah, Ravish. It is."

"Does it make you uncomfortable?"

"No." I laughed. "Hopefully it would take more than a bit of silver to make me uncomfortable."

She brought her coffee, sat beside me, poured creamer, and used my spoon to stir it.

"This is good," I said. "I don't have a toothbrush with me."

She grinned. "Yes. You do. In fact all of your stuff is upstairs."

"All my stuff from the hotel?"

"Uh-huh."

"You were serious about them moving me? You mean they just let anybody walk in and take a guest's belongings?"

"No." She shook her head. "We're not *anybody*."

"I'm starting to get that loud and clear."

"But it's not just your stuff from the hotel. It's your stuff from L.A., too."

"What? Hector let you guys in?"

"Not exactly. He was asleep. Never knew we were there. But we left enough money to cover your part of the rent for a year."

She blew on the hot coffee before she took a sip and the sight of her lips puckering temporarily mesmerized me so that I was having a hard time focusing on the proper amount of outrage.

I shook my head. "How could you have my stuff from L.A.? You couldn't have known I was going to say yes."

She laughed that whore's laugh that turned me inside out like a pretzel. "Well, you're right, of course. But we've been doing these competitions for a very long time and no guy has ever said no."

I cleared my throat, tearing my eyes away from her mouth. "That's quite a record."

"Yeah." She watched me over the top of her cup as she drank.

"What do I need to know about the ceremony tomorrow?"

"Well, there are some old-fashioned things. You and I will wear hooded robes until we ring the bell and snuff out the candle."

"That's probably not any more ridiculous than having fathers 'give brides away' like they were chattel in the twelfth century."

She laughed softly. "The only other thing I need to tell you before the contract is sealed is that witches only conceive daughters. So if you had your heart set on sons, it could be a problem."

There was no mistaking that she was practically holding her breath, waiting for my answer. I laughed out loud. "No, Ravish. I never pictured myself as a father to anybody, girl or boy. And I should probably tell you, I still don't."

She sipped coffee while considering that. "That's not a deal breaker for me, Willem."

"Why not?" My mouth seemed to have gone rogue and been disconnected from the part of me that knew you shouldn't challenge the gift of a horse by closely examining its teeth. Or something like that. But I'd gone too far to pull back. "Why me?"

She set her coffee cup down, slid off the stool, and walked in between where my legs were spread and resting on the rungs. I suddenly became preoccupied with wanting to find out if that kiss was a fluke or if it could be as good as I remembered. I put my hands on her waist and reveled in her body heat as I drew her in closer.

"I wasn't kidding when I said you were made for me, Willem. There are people here who know about such things. Right up to the perfect moment to approach you with an opportunity, the moment when you'd be most receptive to trying something new."

"Like you?"

I slipped my hand under her hair and let it caress her neck. She closed her eyes like she enjoyed the sensation.

"Yes. Like me. But no sex tonight," she said, and pulled away abruptly.

"What? Wait! I was looking forward to that."

She smirked and laughed deep in her throat. "Very gratifying. That means you'll be *really* ready by tomorrow. Tonight you're in one of the guest rooms. Tomorrow when we're gone to the ceremony, the servants will move you in with me."

"Tomorrow's too far away." I pouted. "My dick needs attention tonight."

"Well, I'm sure you can find a way to take care of that. But it will be the last time you'll have to take care of your, um, dick by yourself."

"I like the way you say 'dick'."

"I liked the way you said you were looking forward to sex with me."

"Well, duh."

"Come on," she said. "Tomorrow I want to hear everything about what you'd like to do with your time. Oh, and the winners are giving you some sort of guy thing tomorrow night at dinner, not a bachelor party, but something like that."

"I'd rather be with you."

"Willem, you are charming the socks off me."

"I have it on good authority that you're not wearing socks, but I'd like to charm the rest of this off you." I slid two fingers under the strap of her dress.

"Stop. You're making this hard." She pulled away.

"That's the idea."

"Don't make me put you in time out."

All humor was suddenly sucked out of the room. "Could you do that? No, wait. A better question is probably, would you do that?"

She grew serious. "No, Willem. It was a joke. Something my sister says to her kids. I will never use magic to force, compel, or coerce you. It's not only against the rules. It's wrong."

I heard what she was saying, but the idea that she *could* do that, or thought she could do that, was a little bit concerning and a little bit disturbing.

"So you're saying you could force me to do things," I said slowly, watching closely for her reaction, "but you wouldn't because of an ethics code."

"Yes. That and because I will love you."

"You'll love me," I repeated drily. "How can you know that?"

She blew out a breath like she was getting frustrated. "I keep telling you, Willem. We're perfect for each other. I won't be able to stop myself from being head over heels for you."

"And is that what you're expecting from me? Love?"

"Is that too much to hope for?"

I ran a hand through my hair. "It may be a bridge too far. Love doesn't seem likely. I don't mean because of you," I hastened to add. "I just don't have any history to indicate that I'm a fall-in-love kind of guy."

She was silent for a few seconds. "I guess we'll see then."

I smiled, grateful that she was going to let it go. "I guess we will."

"I'm going up to bed. If you want to come with me, I'll show you where you're staying tonight. Then if you want to wander around, or whatever, feel free. Mi casa es su casa. At least it will be tomorrow."

I followed her up the stairs enjoying the way her hips swayed when she climbed. "Oh, there's an elevator, too, if you're ever feeling lazy."

An elevator?

The second floor hallway ended at double doors standing open. I supposed that was the master. I saw only windows with a console table and lamps.

When we reached the last room on the left, she said, "This is you tonight. Do you want to see our suite?"

"Our suite? Why, yes. I do want to see our suite," I said playfully.

When I reached the threshold, I could see that there was a large sitting area with pale gray carpet, plush white sofas, a fireplace, and a movie-screen size TV. To the left was another set of double doors that stood open to reveal the bedroom, as tastefully done as the rest of the house. I hadn't had an impulse to run leaping and jump up and down on a bed for twenty years, but I had to restrain myself from doing exactly that.

There were doorways with eight-foot doors on either side of the bed.

"That's yours." She pointed to the one on the left.

"This one is mine." She waved a hand at the other door. "Come on. I'll show you yours."

We stepped into an enormous bathroom with black and white marble tiles, turned diagonally, a huge polished black Jacuzzi, a carwash shower with a dozen heads, long black marble sink counter and mahogany stained cabinets. Very masculine and very luxurious. I was pretty sure the oil-rich princes of Saudi Arabia would be jealous.

When she opened tall mahogany doors, lights came on beyond. "This is your closet," she said.

My room in the L.A. apartment was not nearly as big. It had a big island cabinet with drawers on all sides and miles of rods for hung clothes hidden behind tall cupboard doors.

"I take it we're not sharing a bath?"

She giggled. "My sisters tell me that nothing kills romance quicker than a shared bathroom."

I'd never shared a bathroom with a woman, but I could still grasp the point.

"It's marvelous, Ravish. I don't have enough clothes to fill even one of these." I opened one of the tall cupboard doors.

"Well, that could change, Willem. If you decide you want more clothes, you'll have a place to keep them."

"Every few minutes something else leaves me speechless."

She smiled. "Tomorrow, when you're up, let's have breakfast together on the terrace. I want to hear everything about your family, your acting, your life in L.A."

I cocked my head, pleased that she was interested.

"Sure. And you'll reciprocate."

She didn't answer, just smiled, walked toward me and proceeded to kiss me stupid again. Then she patted me on the ass. I'm not joking. She actually patted me on the ass and guided me toward the door. I decided to take that as a promise of things to come. Tomorrow.

"Night," I said, as she closed the double doors.

The crazy idea hit me that perhaps it was some sort of test. Was I supposed to plow through the doors and insist we not wait to consummate our year? I'd been told that some women have fantasies about having their choice taken away, but only by the man of their dreams. I was the man of Ravish's dreams. She'd told me so several times.

It could be a test of patience or a test of impatience and I was having a hard time deciding which. I finally decided I'd rather err on the side of no means no, than err on the side of being perceived as a brute.

So I wandered back down the hall to the room she'd pointed out as my temporary castle. It wasn't bad. Had I not just seen the rooms that would be mine, I would have thought it might be the most outrageously opulent room on Earth. It even had a fully stocked mini bar with snacks in the little refrigerator and a TV almost as big as the one in the master suite. A guy could get used to the lifestyle quick.

The bathroom counter had my toiletries laid out neatly. The clothes that I'd brought to Wimberley were cleaned, pressed, and hung. Undies and socks in the top drawer. Wow. They had good elves in Wimberley.

Popping the top on a long neck ginger ale, I shed everything but my boxers, climbed in bed and turned on the TV. I surfed until I was sure there was nothing worth watching and finally settled on *The Wicker Man*. I would have loved to turn the channel or, better yet, turn the TV off, but I couldn't do it. Consequently, I had a restless night filled with dreams of human sacrifice and worries about what I was really getting myself into.

When I saw light coming through the windows, I was relieved the night was over. I told myself that nothing so sinister was going on in Wimberley or there wouldn't be so many happy winners. On the other hand...

The shower felt good. I set the water on practically scalding and hoped it would wash both doubts and nightmares away. I pulled on a pair of old soft jeans and a grayish blue tee then headed out. When I opened the door, I could hear activity in the kitchen below. Not only that, but I could smell coffee and bacon.

When I stepped into the kitchen, a large middle-aged woman turned to me with a bright smile and said, "Good morning, Mr. Draiocht. Would you like anything special for breakfast?"

"What's your name?"

"Angie, sir."

"Well, Angie. All thought of whatever else I might have wanted fled when I smelled that bacon." She smiled as if she was pleased. "Did I also smell coffee?"

"Oh, yes." She wiped her hands on her apron. "The mistress likes percolated coffee in the morning. So we do it the old-fashioned way. It's not easy to find these old vintage machines now, but they do make good coffee."

A man stepped into the room. "Good morning, Mr. Draiocht."

"Hello," I said. "What's your name?"

"Ed, sir. I'll let Ms. Wimberley know you're up."

"Thank you."

"We've set up for breakfast out on the terrace if that's alright with you," said Angie. "I'll bring your coffee out with some fruit to get you started." She waved in the direction of the terrace behind me.

"Sounds nice."

I smiled as I turned toward the terrace doors. I could see the table set with pink linens and covered carafes of ice water and orange juice. The morning was glorious, a perfect seventy degrees. The smell of cedar scented the air and I inhaled deeply.

Angie followed close behind with the coffee pot. She turned the cup over and poured then carefully set the cream and sweeteners within my reach.

"Lovely morning, isn't it?" she said.

"It is."

The door opened and Ravish emerged, wearing white capris and a tangerine-colored tank top. Her hair was in a ponytail. She looked different in casual clothes. No less beautiful. If anything, she seemed more approachable in everyday street wear. A guy could get used to fancy breakfast served on the terrace and a goddess looking at him like he'd discovered fire.

"Willem," she said.

"Ravish," I replied. "Let's start this off right. Call me Will."

She smiled. "Sure."

"And Ravish has got to go, too."

"You don't like my name?" She didn't seem hurt, more interested in what I would say next.

"I love it, but I have a strong preference for single syllables. I'm a simple kind of guy."

As she sat, she took on a challenging look with raised eyebrow. "A simple kind of guy, huh. I'm not getting that, Wille… Will. Perhaps you haven't had the funds to express your appreciation of fine things, but I'm kind of questioning the simple guy thing."

I wondered if she was right. She might be.

"So what name have you come up with for me?"

I sat back with my coffee cup in hand. "Rave."

"Rave?!? It makes me sound like a soapbox lunatic."

"Ravish makes me sound like a pervert."

She threw her head back and laughed her sexy, throaty laugh. "If you want to call me Rave, it's okay with me, Will. Outsiders will think it's short for Raven, but that's okay, too. I always liked that name."

"Rave it is then."

I felt strangely satisfied, as if I'd just branded my woman by renaming her. It was a rush.

Angie stepped out carrying a tray with two plates of spinach Eggs Benedict, bacon, and gingerbread.

"Good heavenly days," I said. "How did you know I like spinach Eggs Benedict? And gingerbread? Christ. I don't know where to start. It smells like heaven."

"I take that as high praise, Mr. Draiocht."

"You should. This looks incredible."

Angie went away beaming.

"I hope you always enjoy things as much as you do today, Will."

"You mean you don't want me to get bored and jaded? I'm not a teenager. I think I've lived long enough without all this to ever not appreciate it."

"Good," she said. "It's more fun that way. So start at the beginning and tell me everything about you."

After taking a large bite of gingerbread, I grinned. "Only if you trade me fact for fact. I tell one. You tell one."

"Deal. You go first."

"I was born in Alabama."

"I was born here."

"Two brothers and a sister."

"Two sisters."

"I'm the youngest."

"I'm number two."

"I had a nice middle class childhood. My parents weren't the cool parents who let kids do *anything*, but they were solid, stable, loving."

"My parents are," she grinned, "great. I can't wait for you to meet them."

I thought about taking Ravish to meet my parents. "Will you want to meet mine?"

She nodded. "After our year is up. When our arrangement becomes permanent, then yes. Absolutely."

"We could take a road trip. Go through New Orleans. Drive along the Gulf."

Her eyes sparkled when she smiled like she was picturing the sun on the water. "I'm in!"

I couldn't help but return her smile. I could picture driving along the coast with Rave in her Spyder, top down. Heaven.

"Okay. So childhood. I played baseball and, don't tell anybody, but I liked to read."

"I like to read, too, and I guess I was what some people call a tomboy. I always liked hiking, canoeing, catching June bugs."

"You have June bugs?"

"Of course."

I laughed. "For about a week every summer our June bugs would look like one of the plagues from the Bible. There were that many."

"Yeah. We get a lot. I also liked playing in the mud."

"No."

"Yes."

"Okay. Well I would never have admitted that to you, but definitely concur. Playing in the mud is the best!" I held my palm up for a high five. She slapped my hand and giggled.

"Is that why you have that Jeep? You still like to play in the mud?"

She looked up through her eyelashes. "Guilty."

"Well, Rave, I'm feeling pretty good about this. What are the chances I'd find a girl who likes to play in the mud?"

"What subjects did you like in school?"

"Social studies. English when it involved stories. You?"

"Math and science."

I laughed. "Well, between the two of us, there shalt be

balance. How old were you when you had your first kiss?"

"Thirteen."

"Twelve. Did you like it?"

"Not really."

"Yeah." I chuckled. "Awkward."

"Extremely. And don't start asking about other things along those lines. Some things are private, even from you, Will."

"Noooooo. I'm to be your lord and master. You will do as I say." She looked at me strangely. "That was a joke, Rave. I don't expect that you'd ever do what I say even if I was dumb enough to give you an order."

"Okay."

"Seriously. You can keep that stuff to yourself. I was kidding."

"Good," she said as she bit down on a piece of bacon. "I'm glad we understand each other. So when was your first coitus and who was it with?"

My eyes jerked from the hunk of gingerbread I was holding, to her face. Her eyes were dancing. "I have a better question. Are you ticklish?" She pressed her lips together and shook her head a little too emphatically. "Ooh. I just learned two things. You *are* ticklish and you're also a terrible liar. Good. To. Know."

I stood and moved toward her with fingers wiggling. She jumped up and began walking backwards. "No, Will, really. I…"

She feinted left, but though I hadn't revealed it, I also played basketball. So I was ready for her. She ran right into my arms. I was not merciless. After all, I'd known her for less than twenty-four hours. Merciless tickling required history and trust. Sometimes, as my sisters had taught me, there were elements of head bonking with nearby objects that resulted in needing ice packs.

I turned her to face me. "I didn't get a good morning kiss." Without further preamble, she proceeded to kiss me stupid. "Have I told you I like your lips?"

"No." She smiled. "What else?"

"What else what?"

"What else do you like about me?"

"You mean besides flawless beauty? I like your laugh. I like that you're so easy to talk to. I like the way your eyes dance when you're having fun. And I like your Eggs Benedict."

"That was a good starter list, Will. You want to finish breakfast?"

"Hell, yeah. There's stuff all over that table still calling my name. I just took intermission for tickling."

I slid my arm over her shoulder as we walked back. It was familiar. It was affectionate. It was also strange, not the sort of thing I do with women, but it felt natural. And good.

"This gingerbread is getting cold! What kind of household are you managing here?" I chided with enough tease in my voice so she'd know for sure that I was not serious.

Angie appeared at the table within seconds.

"Angie," Rave said, "could you heat up the gingerbread for Mr. Draiocht?"

"Certainly. So glad you like it, sir."

She took the gingerbread basket and hurried away while I sat with my mouth hanging open.

"I wasn't serious."

"Oh, I know. But gingerbread *is* best when the butter melts on it. And Angie doesn't mind."

"How do you know?"

"When she comes back, ask her and look real closely for any signs that she might be shaving the truth."

"You're on, mistress of the house."

While waiting, I scooped up the last bite of incredible Eggs Benedict, polished off the bacon, and gulped orange juice.

"You've got an appetite, Will. I may have to put a weight maintenance spell on you. With your permission, of course."

I stared. "You're saying you can put a spell on me that would allow me to eat anything I want, as much as I want, and not gain weight?" She nodded with a secretive little smile. I reached down and rubbed my hand over my bulging tummy. "Can you make me look shredded without having to work out?"

She laughed. "No. Some things are beyond me. If you want to be lickable, you're still going to have to hit the machines. Oh. I didn't show you the gym. It's upstairs on the right side of the hall. Got everything you could want and a nice media center, too."

"Lickable?"

She giggled. "Is that all you heard?"

"Yes. Blah blah blah. LICKABLE! Blah blah blah. Now you know. That's one of the words that's a cock tease."

"Oh? What are the others?"

"We'll come to that later. Were you popular in school or studious or what? Lots of acquaintances or a few good friends?"

"I was kind of popular, I guess."

Looking down my nose, I said, "What's 'kind of'? Were you a cheerleader?"

"Yes."

"Did you use magic?"

"No." She did a crazy eyes thing that looked like she was indignant at the question.

"Okay. Okay. Just asking. Were you prom queen?"

"No. I was senior class president though."

Angie arrived with warm gingerbread and set it down with a smile.

Watching her carefully I asked, "Angie, don't you really think I should get up and bring the gingerbread in the kitchen if I want it heated up?"

"Good lands no, sir. That's my job, isn't it?"

"Maybe."

"No maybe about it. I see to the people in this house. That used to be Ms. Ravish, but now it's you, too."

"You call her Ms. Ravish?"

"With her permission."

"Why don't you call me Will?"

"Mr. Will."

"No. Just Will." She looked at Rave, who nodded at her. "Very well, sir. But it don't really seem right calling you by your nickname."

"Okay. You can call me Willem. But just you. Nobody

else."

She looked delighted at the prospect of being the only one allowed to call me Willem.

"Very well, sir."

When she left and closed the door behind her, I said, "So you were one of the unattainable sex icons who prowl the halls of high schools everywhere, never deigning to so much as cast a glance toward poor adoring souls such as myself."

"Wow, Will. That was practically a soliloquy. You would have been a fine actor."

"What does math/science girl know about soliloquys?"

"I named my *favorite* subjects. That doesn't mean that I didn't learn anything else."

"Oh, well, see? When I say I liked social studies and stories. I *do* mean I didn't learn anything else."

She laughed. "What about you? Social or kept to yourself?"

"Few good friends. Not the party crowd. Not the jocks. Not the elite-by-virtue-of-daddy's-money circle. Maybe I was a nerd."

"Nerds don't play sports."

"Hmmm. Maybe I defy description. I had a few good friends. I could get dates when I wanted. No complaints really. How old were you when you got your first car?"

"Fourteen."

I laughed. "No. Really."

"Really. I got a hardship license."

"You did? What was the hardship?"

She sat back and bit into a peach. "It would have been

too hard to not be able to drive when I was ready to drive."

I narrowed my eyes at her. "Did you just say that?"

She laughed. "I did."

"And the Department of Motor Vehicles bought that?"

"Well, we didn't use the usual channels."

"Are you used to getting whatever you want, Rave?"

Looking straight at me, she took another bite out of the peach. "Hmmm." She nodded.

"So you're spoiled."

"I don't believe in being spoiled. I think that everybody should be able to enjoy everything they can using the talents they were given. So long as they give back," she added.

"That's an interesting point of view. What's giving back mean to you?"

"Well, I got a car when I was fourteen, but I used it to take schoolwork to kids who were home sick. I also gave rides to people who needed to go to the doctor and stuff."

That did sort of put things in a different light. "So you're a saint disguised as a witch living in the lap of wealth and decadence."

Her mouth dropped open. "There's nothing decadent about the way I live. How dare you?"

I laughed. "Okay. If you say so."

"When did you start driving?"

"Sixteen. Like normal people." She smirked. "My granddad gave me a hand-me-down car when I was sixteen. I think it had two hundred and thirty thousand miles on it. Old sedan painted a color that we called granddad green. It didn't turn the heads of any girls, I promise you, but it got me around and was better than a bicycle."

"So you went to college at Alabama State?"

"For a while. I'm kinda sorry I didn't finish now."

"Did you go for higher education?"

"University of Texas. I know. I know. It's close to home, but there's not a better school anywhere in the world."

"Finish?"

"Yes," she said carefully.

"Oh my God. You finished with honors, didn't you?" She looked embarrassed. "Ravish, what in the world do you want with a loser like me?"

Her eyes flashed. "You're not a loser, Will. You just haven't settled into your stride yet."

Something about the way she became suddenly defensive of me, even if she was defending me from myself, caused a little flutter in my six pack, that I was going to need to maintain myself if I wanted to be lickable. And I definitely wanted to be lickable. I could see myself becoming addicted to her protectiveness. And I could see this being the best year of my life.

What I couldn't see was beyond that. Forever was an abstract I couldn't manage to grasp. So I made a vow to enjoy every day, one at a time.

"So you decided to pursue acting?"

"Yeah. For ten years. It didn't work out. What did you study in school?"

"Geology."

"You did not."

"I did."

"Why?"

"I got interested in the limestone ledges, the layers I could see from the river when I was a kid. Of course all the fossils and dinosaur tracks around here were pretty fascinating, too."

"What do you do with your degree?"

"I keep an eye on things around here. Make sure that modernity isn't interfering with what's best for Mother Nature."

"How do you make sure of that?" She didn't answer, but her eyes sparkled. "Okay. Maybe I'm not ready to know that yet."

"We can't protect the world, but we can protect this little corner of it."

"So what's a typical day like for you?"

"If we don't have any meetings," she rolled her eyes, "I test water samples and make sure that nobody is dumping anything upstream that shouldn't go into a river. I ride up into the hills and make sure that there aren't any yahoos tearing up the land with SUVS or motorbikes, causing erosion, or doing something abominable like chasing jackrabbits until their little hearts burst."

I pushed back from the table, crossed an ankle over a knee and looked at her. "People do that?"

The tiniest wrinkle appeared between her brows when she frowned. "Yes. People do that."

"So you're like the rabbit sheriff around these parts."

She smiled. "I could do worse than a title like that." I crossed my arms over my chest and felt pretty good about myself, until she said, "And what is your typical day going to look like?"

"One day I was an actor with a routine that involved an agent, auditions, and bartending. The next day I gave up acting and was on a plane for Wimberley, not sure why I was coming here or what I would get out of it." I looked at her, letting her see my appreciation full force. "I never expected you."

"Why, Will," she looked delighted, "that was a nice thing you just said."

I looked away, not wanting to get too mushy. "So I don't have a typical anything right now."

"Let me rephrase the question. What would you like your typical day to be?"

"In bed with you calling me the lord and master of sex?"

She gave me the full sexy laugh treatment, which meant I needed to adjust my pants. "Besides that."

"Since you didn't say no, I'm going to take that to mean that lots of time in bed with you calling me the lord and master of sex is a distinct possibility."

"I don't know about 'lots', but there's some flexibility in my schedule. Lord and master of sex is a pretty serious title. I'm going to expect you to earn it."

"I accept the challenge. Do we get a honeymoon?"

"You mean away from here? After our first year."

"Okay. How much time can we have alone in the house with nobody ringing doorbells or expecting you to be somewhere?"

"Will, I think you're a little bit romantic."

"Think what you like. They call it horny where I come from."

"The answer is yes. We can have a day to ourselves. No interruptions."

"I need to go to Austin."

"Why?"

"Because I'm pretty sure there aren't enough condoms in this town."

"Doesn't matter. You're not going to need them."

"No?"

"No. We're both clean and I'm not getting pregnant unless I want to."

"You just made it even harder to wait for tonight. You sure we can't sneak a preview. Like right now?"

"Yes. I'm sure. Back on topic. What do you want to do? You want to go back to school? We can get you into U.T. If you don't want to study anything but myths and paranormal, they can put together an ad hoc degree tailor made for you."

The idea of going back to school to learn what I wanted to learn without the other crap had me salivating.

"Would it hurt anybody? Would I be taking something away from somebody more deserving?"

"No, Will. The amount of money we donate to that school every year is astronomical. We practically make up for the oil shortfall and we don't ask for much in return. When an opportunity presents itself to repay us, they're more than happy to make an accommodation. You could start in January. Fall's already underway. But you could spend the time planning your degree. You could also get access to a whole bunch of stuff that might not have been available before."

"That's a pretty astounding offer."

"There's just one thing."

"What is it?"

"You can't tell people about us. I mean apart from the obvious. You can't tell people that there are real witches living in Wimberley."

"Betray you?" I started shaking my head. "No. I wouldn't."

"Good to hear. Good to know."

"So what would you like to do until it's time for your induction?"

"Induction?"

"Oh, that's what they call the thing the guys do before the ceremony. Don't get all excited thinking they're going to have strippers. The last guy who tried to sneak one in got caught by his wife and ended up spending the next year as a frog."

I dropped my chin and looked at her. "Is that witch humor? I mean, you're not serious?"

"Don't worry, Will. I'm not the excitable sort. I wouldn't make you live as a frog longer than a fortnight."

"That would be funnier if I was one hundred percent positive that you couldn't do it. Or wouldn't."

She laughed, which was not especially comforting.

What was I getting myself into?

"You want to go out for a drive? See some of the local scenery?"

"Sure." I got to my feet thinking that would be the perfect thing to get my mind off Wicker Man and frogs.

We headed to the garage where I'd seen her Jeep Wrangler 4x4 the night before. It was gorgeous and polished to a sheen.

"This color is really something."

"Fire red metal flake. It looks like the fiberglass dune buggies used to, doesn't it?"

Honestly I couldn't say. "Doesn't look like it's seen much mud."

"Oh, it's seen incredible mud. But it's also seen Ed on a daily basis. He keeps it looking like this and I don't make that easy for him. He even has a machine that cleans the undercarriage in the next bay over."

"That's impressive."

"Yes. Life is good." She pulled herself up into the Jeep, which was open, the canvas top set aside in the garage, opened the bay door and pulled out into the November sunshine.

"Wow. If I thought this color was beautiful inside, that's nothing compared to what it looks like out here with the light shining on it."

"Yeah. It's pretty, huh?"

"Understated. Extremely understated."

"I have to admit that I'm not big on understatement. I like red."

The gates opened as we approached. The attendant gave Ravish a friendly salute as we drove by.

"Why do you need an attendant if you have magic?"

"It's just for show. We don't like to flaunt the magic."

"Oh."

We turned up into the hills away from town, with Rave downshifting expertly. We were still on a narrow, two lane paved road, but the ride was so bumpy, I couldn't imagine what it felt like off road.

"Hey," she yelled over the wind noise. "Let's go to Lookout Mountain. We'll have to climb a lot of stairs, but we had a big breakfast, right?"

Her enthusiasm was so infectious, I was powerless to do anything but nod and smile.

"I need to save some energy for lap dances. You know, in case there are strippers."

She rewarded me with a laugh so hearty I knew it reached down all the way to her pussy. And I laughed with her.

She pulled into a tiny parking lot and put the emergency brake on.

"You want a water?" she asked and then answered her own question. "Yeah. You need a water." She pulled open an ice chest in the back that was stocked with all kinds of stuff, including waters. She pulled one out and tossed it to me.

"Okay, flatlander. Let's see if you've got some muscle tone in those shapely legs."

I hurried to catch up. "Did you just call my legs shapely?"

"I did," she said, already four steps from the bottom.

"I've changed my mind. I'm just going to stay here and watch your heart-shaped ass sway back and forth all the way to the top."

"Come on." She smirked. "The view of my ass is better

up close."

Jesus. I liked this girl.

"Well, alright then," I said as if it would be a chore to walk to the top of the hill with her.

Thirty minutes and one water bottle later, I was enjoying a very fine view of the surrounding Hill Country.

When she pointed, I followed her line of sight. "We own all the land from there to there."

"What do you do with it?"

"We don't do anything with it. That's the point. Well, except for a few goats. They take care of themselves. Pretty much. I guess you could call it a wildlife preserve. No hunting except in cases of necessity."

"What would be a case of necessity?"

"Sometimes the deer population will get too big. When that happens it threatens the survival of all of them. A few have to be thinned out so that the rest can thrive."

"Oh."

"Every now and then we get a mountain lion straying up from Big Bend." That had me kind of looking over my shoulder. She laughed. "Don't worry, Will. You're making far too much noise to be of interest to a big cat."

"Well, that's comforting. Wish we'd brought two waters."

"Race you back down."

It took thirty minutes to climb up and five minutes to run down. I made it to the ice chest first and felt like thumping my chest. Me man. Stronger. Faster. But I was gentlemanly enough to toss her a water before taking one for myself.

"This is probably a silly question, but are you hungry?" she asked.

"Did you see how many steps I just climbed? Yes. Of course I'm hungry!"

She giggled. Looking at her smartwatch she said, "The best taco truck in Texas stops by the river right about now, just a little ways from here. Sound good?"

"Taco truck? I don't know."

"Trust me. They're clean as the Four Seasons."

"Well, with a vouch like that…"

"Let's go."

Fifteen minutes later we were sitting on a picnic bench under an ancient cypress tree scarfing down what could possibly be the best tacos in the world.

"Ah. This food is good! I mean it's goooooood." She hummed agreement around her own bite of spicy yumminess. "Will it embarrass you if I go back for more?"

She snorted. "No. Why would it?"

I took a sip of IBC root beer out of an ice cold longneck bottle. "Where does the money come from?"

"Oh. Well, there wasn't a lot until the early nineteen hundreds. You know we're kind of a haven for witches. They began coming from all over. One of them had a gift for the stock market. Even managed to pull out ahead of the crash and then buy back in. I'm not one of the treasurers, but I'm told that, once you get something like that established, it takes on a life of its own. Starts producing money like bamboo spreads.

"And since we live in a cooperative, everybody shares. There's plenty to go around. So we each use our own talents to the best advantage of the community." She shrugged. "It works out."

"By all appearances, it certainly does. So what's your special talent?"

She grinned. "You sure you're ready for this?"

"You're scaring me."

"No, no, silly. There's no reason to be scared. I have a gift for astral projection."

"Wow."

"You know what it is?"

"I do."

"Yeah. Cool, huh?"

"I don't know. How do you use it?"

"Well, if we need to know what's going on somewhere in the world, I can find out without being seen or heard. Nobody ever knows I was there."

Tacos all but forgotten, I studied her to see if she really believed what she was saying. "So you're a fly on the wall."

"I guess you could say that. Although that doesn't sound as glamorous as invisible spy."

"Can I get a demonstration?"

"You doubt me, Will?"

"Come on. Make me a believer. Just a little one."

"Okay. Make a proposal."

"Tell me what my mother is doing right now."

"We have to go home. I can't do it out in the open because I, you know, I have to leave my body." She whispered that last part. "It's not that I doubt that you'd watch over me, but it's easier to be safe in my safe room at home."

"You have a safe room?"

"We have a safe room."

"I keep forgetting. Just give me a few days to adjust to thinking of everything that's yours as being ours."

"No problem."

"So let's go."

She looked at my uneaten tacos. "You were talking about getting more tacos. You haven't even finished those. Are you upset?"

I shook my head. "No. Just eager. Maybe a little excited."

"You sure? Your mother will still be there if you enjoy your tacos first."

Standing up, I said, "This experiment is even more fun than tacos." Then I grabbed one of the untouched tacos and started eating it as I was walking back to the Jeep.

"Okay." She shook her head, but got up, gathered the garbage, threw it in the receptacle and met me at the Jeep.

I swung into the passenger side, still holding my IBC, and gave her an encouraging smile.

Yes. I lied.

I wasn't excited.

I was nervous.

Part of me wanted to find out she was the real deal. Part of me was terrified to find out she was the real deal. And part of me was worried she might be an ordinary everyday heiress with delusions of supernatural powers. Best to find out before the ceremony.

"When's your birthday?" I asked to pass the time.

"October fourteenth."

"I just missed it. How old were you?"

"Twenty-six."

"What did you do to celebrate?"

"Danced naked in the moonlight." When I looked to see if she was serious, she laughed. "Just kidding. We gave up cavorting with the devil centuries ago when we figured out there wasn't any devil to cavort with." It was my turn to snort. "Went to Sixth Street in Austin with friends. Listened to music. Got half plastered.

"I know when your birthday is."

I smiled. "Oh yeah?"

"December thirteenth. It adds up to my lucky number, seven."

"How do you figure that December thirteenth adds up to seven?"

"If somebody asks for the month and day of your birth, what do you say?"

"Twelve thirteen."

"So picture that number in your mind like you would write it down. One, two, slash, one, three. You add up the numbers. One plus two plus one plus three equals seven."

The smirk just couldn't be helped. "You're a superstitious witch, aren't you?"

She laughed. "So what do you want for your birthday?"

"You naked popping out of a cake in our bedroom."

Her eyes slid sideways to take me in. "I hope that's always your answer, Will."

CHAPTER SIX

T HE SAFE ROOM was pretty impressive. State of the art. It was equipped to defend against just about anything from tornadoes to body snatchers. That last part addressed Rave's fear about astral projection, that someone could hurt her while her spirit was away from her body. I think we were probably more secure in that room than we would have been if we accidentally got locked inside Fort Knox. One thing was for sure. She took this stuff seriously.

There was a big overstuffed chair in there along with shelves of candles and curios. I sat on a cushion on the floor with my back to the wall while she sat on the chair.

"I'm going to need some clues as to where to look for your mother, Will. Give me an address. Tell me what the house looks like and what she looks like."

"I haven't seen her for a couple of years. So she might have changed her hair. Women do that. But she used to wear it cut to about here." I made a motion just above my shoulder. "It's dark brown like mine. At least it was the last time I saw her. She's average height and weight. Mid-fifties and she hasn't had any work done, that I know of. 47 Fig Avenue in Fairhope. It's Sunday afternoon. So she's probably home."

"Okay." She smiled. "Be right back. There's only one rule. Don't touch me while I'm gone."

"What would happen?"

"I might lose the connection. And not get back."

For some reason that raised the hairs on the back of my neck and I was sorry I'd asked her to do something dangerous for such a frivolous reason.

"Wait!" I practically yelled. "It's not worth it. I didn't know there was a possibility of… that."

"Don't worry, Will. As long as you don't touch me, everything will be fine. See you in a few."

At that she was gone. How did I know she was gone? Because all the light went out of her body. She didn't exactly look gray and she didn't exactly look dead, but she definitely didn't look like anybody was home. The glow that shone from her was missing. Her arms rested on the plush furniture. Her head had dropped so that her chin was against her chest.

It seemed that I could rule out delusion. I wasn't sure that I could name what was happening, but it was *something*. There was nothing to do but slump back against the wall and wait.

About five minutes later I heard a whoosh sound. Ravish took in a deep breath, raised her head, and the light came back into her body. Then she laughed out loud.

"Your mother is a hoot, Will. She's giving some handsome guy, who I'm guessing is your dad, what for about flowers. She wants them to stay where they are. He wants to move them somewhere because they draw bees and the bees are a nuisance."

I pulled my cell phone out of my pocket. "Will I get reception in here?"

"Of course. It wouldn't be a safe room if you couldn't call out."

I thumbed my mother's phone number and put it on speaker.

"Hello?" she said.

"Mom?"

"Will! Great heavenly days, I can't believe I'm hearing your voice." Her excitement quickly switched to concern. "Is everything alright?"

"Everything's good, Mom. More than good. I need to ask you something and it's real important. I know this is a strange question, but I need you to tell me what you're doing right now, this very minute."

"Well, if you must know, I'm having a knockdown, drag out argument with your father. He's moving my peonies to the back fence because he doesn't like the bees. Ridiculous! Mark Twain said that if there are no bees there is no food and that's the end of us all."

"Are you sure that was Mark Twain?"

"No, but I don't have time to look it up. I'm trying to save my peonies from your lunatic of a father."

I was watching Rave's eyes glitter above her smug expression the entire time my mother was talking.

"Mom. I love you. Guess what? I have a girlfriend."

"No. That's not possible."

"Yeah. Live in and everything."

"You have to bring her home! What's she like? Can she cook?"

"She's a marvel in so many ways. Oh, and hey. I'm moving to Wimberley, Texas."

"What? What happened to acting?"

"Going back to school."

"Best news I've heard in forever."

"I have to go, but I'll text you the address."

"Don't forget."

"No. I won't. Bye."

"Wait. What's her name?"

"Rave."

"Rave. Short for Raven. Lovely. Talk soon."

I set the phone down. "So you're the real deal."

She raised a perfectly shaped eyebrow. "And I'm your live-in girlfriend?"

"What should I have told my mother? That I'm under contract for a year?"

"Good point. Live-in girlfriend is close enough."

She rose from the chair and stretched her body out, something I could watch again and again without getting tired of it.

"I spent my whole life hoping for proof that the supernatural is real. And here you are."

"Here I am. Rock you like a hurricane."

"What?"

"You didn't ask me what kind of music I like. And considering how much *you* like music, I find that odd."

"You're right. That's probably the first question I should have asked. So what's the answer?"

"I like most American music. Not a huge fan of country. I like bands more than karaoke-style pop singers. I guess I'm a rock chick at heart."

"The era is passing."

"I know." She sighed. "But that's what recorded music is for, right? And there's some surprisingly good new music even if it's harder to find than it used to be."

"Damn Spotify and find-the-singer shows."

"Hear. Hear."

"Have you heard Alabama Shakes?"

"No, but I like the name." I smiled.

"Let's get out of here. I'm getting claustrophobic."

She punched in the code and the door opened with a hiss.

"Is that the house you grew up in?"

"Yeah."

"Nice. Homey."

"Well, we could tear this thing down. Build two thousand square feet of nice hominess."

"Would you like that?"

"No, Rave. I'm teasing. Your house is the second best part of this arrangement."

"I'm thirsty. I always come back thirsty."

"That can be fixed."

We got wine coolers and decided to settle in the study. I walked around looking at the books on the shelves while she watched and sipped her drink.

"Tell me about some of the other special talents. So far I know about predicting stock market trends and astral projection."

"After tonight."

"Why after tonight?"

"Before you learn any more incriminating stuff, I need to know you're committed. To me. To our secrets."

"For a year."

As soon as I saw the look on her face, I felt a pang of regret for restating the condition, but I needed to make it crystal clear up front. I was committing to a year. No more.

"Yes. For a year," she repeated.

CHAPTER SEVEN

HARMONY ARRIVED AT Rave's, I mean… *our* house, a few minutes before I was to leave for the boys-only dinner because it was at Raider's house. Supposedly no witches allowed. Rave told me to take the Spyder and gave directions how to get there. Turn left from the drive, circle around the hill, take the second left and climb until I could see redwood timber and stone.

Raider's house couldn't have been more different from the two houses I'd been in so far. It looked like a northwest pacific lodge with an A-roofline in the center where the front door was prominent and wings jutting out on either side. My first thought was that it suited Raider perfectly.

I followed the circular drive and pulled up to the front where I could see two valet parkers waiting.

"Good evening, Mr. Draiocht."

I was sure I'd never get used to being called by name by strangers, much less being called 'Mr. Draiocht'.

"Hey. This is the place, huh?"

"You're in the right place, sir. We'll take good care of your car."

Leaving the key in the ignition, I said, "Thank you," got out and walked to the door.

Someone who appeared to be staff opened the door as I approached.

"Good evening, Mr. Draiocht. Follow this hallway to the end and take a right. Everyone is outside. You'll hear the music."

"Thank you," I said, thinking 'follow the yellow brick road'.

By the time I was halfway down the hall I could hear the thump of metal bass. The terrace was covered with terrazzo stone in a pinkish reddish color that matched the feel of the house. And it was immense. I suspected there were fifty guys there, but it would have accommodated two hundred.

There were three very long tables set for dinner, arranged parallel to each other and perpendicular to the head table. Off to the side, at the very edge of the terrace were two huge built-in grills that formed the center part of a luxurious outdoor kitchen. Two guys in chef gear were grilling steaks. There's no way to adequately convey the aroma, but if you've ever been in the vicinity of steaks being grilled to perfection out of doors, you know what I'm talking about.

I heard Kellan's voice before I saw him. "Man of the hour!"

Everybody stopped and turned to raise their drinks to me. I raised my chin and smiled, a little embarrassed to be the center of attention. Strange reaction for a would-be actor, right?

Raider came over and slapped me on the shoulder almost hard enough to knock me over. "How you doin', hero?"

I suspected that would always get a smile out of me. "I was pretty good before you tried to start a fight."

He guffawed at that. "Willem, you're one of a kind."

"Call me Will."

"Will it is then." Kellan strolled up. "You've met Kellan."

"I have." Kellan and I were shaking hands in greeting when a waiter showed up by my side to ask about a drink. After a double take, I said, "Roque! Roque Quintanilla!"

The man looked both proud and pleased that I remembered him. "Yes, Mr. Draiocht. What will it be my pleasure to bring you? Margarita? On the rocks, no salt, Jose Reposado?"

I laughed. "You have an incredible memory."

"As do you, sir."

"Hmmm. Well, tonight I've got the nerves of a virgin groom. I'm going with whiskey neat."

"Very good, sir. We have…"

I held up my hand. "I trust you, Roque. Bring me what you think I'd like."

After a smile and a head nod, he disappeared.

"Nerves of a virgin groom," Raider repeated with a belly laugh. "I suspect whiskey will help out with that."

"So who have you met?" Kellan asked.

"Just the two of you and Simon."

"Simon?!?" They both asked it at the same time and then shared a glance.

"Is there something wrong with Simon?"

"Uh, no," said Raider. "He's alright, but he's not what

you'd call…"

"…outgoing." Kellan finished the sentence. "Keeps to himself."

"Is he here tonight?"

"No. He doesn't usually come to these things."

"What exactly is this? Ravish said it's kind of like a bachelor party, but not."

"It's a chance to introduce you around. Don't worry about not remembering everybody's names. That'll come in time," Kellan said.

"So, if Simon isn't here, that means there are probably others who aren't here?"

He nodded. "There are about twenty or so others. Mostly old guys. They'll be at the ceremony, of course, but going out twice in one day is too much for some people."

"Save me from that day," Raider said.

"No worries. You'll never make it to fifty," Kellan told Raider.

"Good. Just as well," he said. "I'm going to supervise dinner. I have a lot of experience with cooking meat outdoors." I didn't doubt that for an instant. "Catch up with you later."

"Raider!" He stopped and turned around. "Really nice house."

He gave a cautious smile, like he wasn't accustomed to being complimented on his house, and a chin dip before resuming his mission to 'supervise' the cooking.

"Come on," Kellan said. "Get ready to press some flesh."

He wasn't kidding about shaking hands with a lot of

dudes. He also wasn't kidding about the fact that I had no hope of remembering their names. It wasn't just the aroma of steaks grilling to perfection that had me grateful when Raider shouted, "Dinner!"

"This way," Kellan said.

I followed him to the head table. Three guys were already seated. I assumed one of them was the other inductee. Kellan gestured to the chair that was in the middle of the remaining three. Kellan sat down to my right. Raider appeared from nowhere and sat to my left.

It was beginning to get dark so the gathering was lit with tiki torches and an extremely generous distribution of candles on the tables.

Like the barbeque, we each had two iced carafes of sweet tea and water. The waiters began making their way down the rows, delivering plates. What was on my plate was an extra large filet mignon, butterflied, and cooked medium well, more well than medium. Just the way I like it.

I turned to Kellan. "This is my favorite."

His blue eyes twinkled with amusement. "By the time you get this far, they know everything about you, Will."

"I don't know whether to be flattered or creeped out."

"This time next week I'll remind you that you said that. We'll see how you feel by then."

My plate also held an enormous Idaho potato wrapped in foil. A waiter appeared on my left, grabbed my potato and smushed several times using a pristine white towel. He then opened the foil, cut it down the middle, and asked what I would like from the variety of goodies on his two-tiered condiment server.

"Butter." He gave me two spoonfuls. "More," I said and he added another spoonful. "Bacon bits. Cheddar cheese. Little bit of sour cream. Not much. Perfect."

When he turned away, another waiter took his place. "Green beans almondine, sir?"

"Yeah. Sure." He scooped them up with tongs and laid them on the platter so that they were photograph-ready.

I was offered several more vegetables, but decided there was enough in front of me already even though my girlfriend could keep me from gaining weight. Yeah. It sounded funny to say that even in my head, but even though that was a perk beyond compare, she couldn't keep me from being uncomfortable as the result of obscene eating, otherwise known as gluttony.

The men seemed to be chatting amiably over dinner.

"So I'm the guest of honor?" I said to Kellan.

"Indeed you are one of two as you will be again at the end of the year."

"So what do I need to know about community politics?"

"What do you mean?"

"It hasn't escaped my notice that you're more or less in charge."

Kellan laughed. "Well, I wouldn't call that politics exactly. Glory and I both like entertaining. I get along with people. They get along with me. It just kind of happened naturally."

"Naturally." I repeated. "You just ended up with that castle naturally?" He laughed again. "I know there's a chance that could have sounded like envy. Believe me, it's nothing of the sort. I'm wandering around in Rave's house as it is."

"Rave?"

"Uh, yeah. That's what I call her."

He smiled as he took a bite of his New York strip. "Okay."

"Anyway I don't want your house, but I'm curious as to how things work."

"In a cooperative like this one, things have a way of working out the way they should. People take on tasks according to their own talents and, mysterious as it may seem, everybody ends up liking their role, the way they fit in."

"Very Utopian."

"Well, money helps give us the freedom to pursue our own interests. It makes it possible for us to hire phenomenal help who take on the aspects of living that are more drudgery. Not going to lie about it. In many ways that's the best thing of all."

I nodded. "Yeah. I see that. Rave has this amazing cook named Angie who makes gingerbread I'd die for. And this guy named Ed. I'm not sure what all he does yet, but he keeps the mud off her Jeep so that it always looks like it's sitting in a showroom."

"Somethin' else," Raider said from the other side of me. "You know that Bible thing about coveting your neighbor's wife?"

"The commandment? Yeah. You don't come from a state like Alabama without hearing about such things."

"That's not a problem here. You're going to find that, no matter how beautiful the other women are, the only one you're gonna want is your own." He grinned. "Nice how that works out. Keeps everybody happy. Male and female. Just like it should be."

"They put a spell on us?"

Kellan and Raider looked puzzled by that, but Kellan answered. "Truthfully I don't know, but I also don't care. Happy is happy." He smiled. "You know what I mean?"

"Well…"

Kellan stood up before I could say more. "Gentlemen, we're here tonight to welcome two new members to what is, perhaps, the most elite fraternity in the world. Cairn Connelly and Willem Draiocht. By the way, he prefers 'Will'.

"Tonight they will take the first step which, of course, all of us remember with fondness because it was the beginning of Earth's best version of a life. In other words, it doesn't get any better than this.

"The men who are gathered here tonight, your future friends and neighbors, want to extend our hearty congratulations on winning the best prize in the known universe. If you think that's exaggeration, you're wrong and will soon know it."

There was a smattering of laughter and agreement.

"Now I'm going to sit down and let our host say a couple of words about Will."

Raider stood up, slapped his big right paw on my left shoulder, and said, "I wish I had a recording of what happened when I took the contestants out on the river. As you know, I like to turn canoes over now and then. I think it builds character.

"Well, knowing Will was one of the winners, I took my measure of him and decided he needed a dunking. So shortly after lunch I made my way through the water with him in my sights. Things didn't go the way I expected. It was like he knew what I was going to do. Just when I was within striking distance, he shoved his paddle under my canoe and tipped me over."

Raider waited through the gasps and following laughter.

"Yep. There I was in the river. So, on a wild hare, I decided to see what would happen if I pretended I couldn't swim." That brought a round of laughter, much louder than the first. I assumed that meant that he was known for being a good swimmer. "So I flailed around in the water and cried for help."

He stopped and looked at me fondly. "There were twenty four contestants on the river that day. Only one of them jumped in to save me. Willem was pulling off his life preserver when he jumped, so that he could offer it to me."

Raider shook his head. "That's why I call him 'hero'. He knew I was a whole hell of a lot bigger and that I was likely to take us both under, but he didn't hesitate to step off the canoe and take me on in the water.

"I gotta tell you. I was impressed. Of course that didn't mean that I could let him get away with dumping my ass in the water. I have a reputation to protect. So I had to dunk him within an inch of drowning." He smiled at me. "But it was all in good fun. Right, Willem?"

I realized that every eye was on me and waiting for an answer to that question. I hesitated for a second, debating about whether or not to tell the truth. "No, Raider. There was nothing fun about it. If I had it to do over, I'd let you drown."

Everybody laughed, no one more than Raider.

"Well, I may have to rethink your nickname then, hero."

When Raider sat down, the guy to the right of Cairn stood up and recounted a couple of references to interesting points in his biography. I was grateful that I'd had Raider to say something more entertaining.

When he was finished, Kellan stood up again. "In a few minutes we'll be taking the boys to the ready rooms. You know the drill. Make them feel welcome whenever you see them out and about and don't be surprised if they don't remember your name at first."

Kellan sat down and said, "Eat up," then with lowered voice and a grin. "You're going to need your energy later."

I looked at my plate, still half full, and agreed that, whatever was coming next, I didn't want to be distracted by hunger. That wouldn't normally be an issue for me. I supposed there must be some magical property in the Wimberley air to put me on the verge of ravenous half the time.

Giving my plate my full attention, I set to work finishing the feast of kings that had been set before me. When my favorite bar man brought me a third drink, Kellan put his arm between Roque and me then shook his head. The drink turned around and went the other way along with

Roque.

"Hey," I said. "I'm on a two-drink maximum?"

"Yes. You're signing a contract tonight and it's the most important contract you'll ever enter into. This is not a frat party hazing, Will. It's serious as can be and it doesn't count if you're not sober."

"I'm sober!" I protested.

He pinned me with a blue-eyed stare. "As. A. Judge."

Seeing that he meant what he said, I decided to get on board. "Okay, then. Not trying to cause trouble."

"Yeah. You say that now, but I can already see that you're going to try to shake things up every chance you get."

"Me? No. You got it wrong. I'm not the rebel type."

Kellan barked out a laugh. "Whatever you say. If you're done with that plate, we're moving on to the next step."

"We as in you and me?"

"Yes. And Raider."

"Should I expect to be punked?"

Kellan chuckled. "Not tonight. Like I said, this is *serious* stuff."

"Okay. So where are we going and what are we going to do?"

"We're going back to my house, which is where the ceremony will be. You and Raider and I are going to hang out in the east wing with non-alcoholic beverages, while we give you the rundown on what to expect tonight and get you ready." My eyes flicked from Kellan to Raider and he smiled. "Think of us as your best men. We both asked for the honor."

"Well," I said slowly, "thank you. That was nice of you."

"It's more than just tonight. We'll be your backup if you have questions about living with a witch. No matter how enthralling they are, there's usually a period of adjustment."

I looked between the two. "I might have some questions about that now."

Kellan exchanged a look with Raider. "Not surprised. I was kind of expecting that. Let's go."

"Rave's car…"

"It'll be waiting for you at my front door after the ceremony."

"Okay."

KELLAN'S RIDE WAS a Range Rover custom long-wheel base. Raider rode shotgun and I was in back, but there was enough room to stretch legs out straight. Or to fit somebody Raider's size comfortably.

The ride to Kellan's house was less than three minutes. We could have walked. Easily.

"So, Will," Raider said, "you ride?"

Running through the possibilities of what that might mean from Raider's perspective, I assumed we were talking motorcycles. "Never have. I'm pretty sure I'd crash into a wall before getting out of first gear."

Raider lifted one huge shoulder in a shrug. "Happens."

With that kind of reassurance, I would be changing my status to 'never will'.

We pulled around Kellan's massive manor house and entered one of six garage bays at the rear.

I opened the door and stepped out onto a smooth shiny, brick-colored floor that looked like it had been waxed a hundred times.

"What is this?" I said, looking at my feet.

"Oh," Kellan said, "it's a kind of new thing. Cool, isn't it?"

"Yeah, cool."

Raider had walked on through the back door like he owned the place. I followed the two of them through the house as Kellan extended cordial greetings to every staff member we passed.

"Mr. MacNamee!" someone called. Kellan stopped and waited as an officious-looking man hurried up to him in a tux. "Everything is prepared according to instruction except that there were so many respondents we can't fit the children's tables in the main room. We can open the doors to the dining hall so that there's not a barrier between the children and their parents. Will that work?"

"Who's supervising the kids?"

"Madame LaBeau."

"Sure. That will be fine. Kids don't care if they're in the main room or not. They just want to be with the other kids."

"Very good, sir."

As the man hurried off, I was thinking, *How bad can it be if they have children's tables?*

"This way," Kellan prompted me to follow.

We made our way to a large comfortable study with

burgundy leather couches, dark wood floors and walls of built-in bookcases, several Remington bronze statues displayed around the perimeter of the room on pedestals and a bar with Ernest Hemingway-style leather bar stools. Very masculine. Very comfortable.

"Wow. You have a bar in your study."

"One of the room's best features, but you're on sissy beverages until after the ceremony. Raider and I will do the same as a show of solidarity."

"It won't bother me if you drink."

"Well, in that case," said Raider.

"No." Kellan gave him a look. "It won't kill us to be fully lucid for a couple of hours."

Raider grumbled something unintelligible.

"Would you like water, soft drink, coffee?" asked Kellan.

"Now that you mention it, coffee sounds good. You have a machine back there."

"Oh yeah. Coming right up."

"So what do I need to know about the proceedings?"

I sat down on one of the barstools as Kellan began brewing coffee. "Well, as you know, two couples will be giving vows tonight."

"Vows?" I don't know why that word alarmed me, but it sounded way too permanent. "I thought this was a promise for a year."

"It is." Kellan gave me a funny look, as did Raider. "The vows cover such things as being exclusive with each other and pledging secrecy regarding what you learn about the community."

"And what is that?"

Kellan set a steaming coffee mug on the bar. "You take cream? Sweetener?"

"Yes. Both, please."

He set a carton of half and half on the bar along with an assortment of artificial sweeteners, white refined, and brown raw sugars. I dumped raw sugar and cream into the cup, stirred, and carried it to one of the sofas.

"I think you already know the answer to that. Magic is real. It happens here."

"Succinct."

"Is that a compliment?"

I laughed. "Maybe."

"The other couple will go first." Kellan sat down on the other sofa facing me. Raider sat in an oversized chair that formed part of the conversation area. "They'll sign their names in their book, recite their vows, snuff out the candle and ring the bell."

"I heard about that. Frankly, it sounds silly."

"Think what you want," Kellan said. "It's one of the old traditions they've kept. I think it makes them feel connected to the past. The old ways."

Nodding, I took a sip. "You make a good cup of coffee."

"No trick to it nowadays, but thanks anyway."

"Raider," I said, "you seem really quiet."

"Kellan can talk enough for four people. I'm here to have your back. Not a lot needs to be said about that."

"Well. Thank you."

"Don't mention it."

"You were saying the other couple will go first?" I asked Kellan.

"Yes. There's really not much to this. You do need a special outfit. We have your clothes in that bag right there."

I followed his eyes and saw that there was a black hanging bag. "What's in there?"

"Black suit. And a hooded robe."

"Hooded robe," I repeated drily.

"Yes. You both, meaning you and Ravish, will wear robes with hoods pulled down so that you can't see each other's faces until after you've spoken the vows. You'll snuff out the candle, ring the bell, take off the robes that symbolize your former life as individuals then kiss."

"Sounds easy enough."

"After that you leave and get on with enjoying your prize while everybody else stays and enjoys champagne."

"I definitely get the better part of that deal."

Kellan smiled. Raider sniggered.

"So what insider tips are you going to give me about how to please my prize?"

"Since each prize is different, you're on your own. Just trust that you wouldn't have won if it wasn't the right thing for both of you. You're a matched pair. You couldn't stop yourself from loving her."

"Love?" I might have sounded a tad alarmed. "I'm not promising that, am I?"

"No. There's no language about love in the vows." Kellan gave me one of his stone-cold serious looks. I was beginning to be able to read him. "You're not afraid of love, are you, Will?"

"Afraid? No. I wouldn't say afraid is the right word. I just don't think love figures in my future because I don't think it's real."

"I see." Kellan exchanged glances with Raider. "Well, stranger things have happened in Wimberley."

"How strange?"

"It would take all the fun out of getting to know the place if we started telling tales."

"Tales? Or eye-witness accounts?"

"We've both seen our share of things we once believed impossible." Kellan pointed a remote at the wall. Book cases slid back to reveal a giant flat screen TV. "You like sports, Will?"

"Not as much as people who go to games or sports bars, but to an extent, yes."

"What kind of sports do you like to watch?"

"Hockey. The last ten minutes of basketball. The U.S. Open."

Raider laughed. "How about canoeing?"

"Well, yeah. I like doing stuff more than watching stuff."

"We've got half an hour to kill before it's time for you to get dressed. What do you want to do?"

"See what's on the History channel?"

Kellan grinned. "Okay."

As it turned out, *All Star Pawn Las Vegas* was doing a rerun marathon and that delighted Raider.

"This show is great!" he pronounced. "Those guys know everything in the world!"

I'd never seen it before, but by the end, I had to admit I was impressed with how much encyclopedic knowledge the owners could regurgitate at a moment's notice.

When it was over, Kellan said, "Time to get ready."

"I'm gonna watch another one," Raider said.

Kellan handed me the hanging bag, which was a lot heavier than it looked. He opened a door to a large bath with dressing area. "We'll help you with the robe. Just get yourself into the suit."

"I guess it's a sure fit."

Kellan smiled. "You're learning. That suit will fit you like it was custom made in Hong Kong."

With that he closed the door.

I looked at myself in one of the full length mirrors and wondered, for the umpteenth time, if I knew what I was doing. The answer was no. I did not know what I was doing, but it was just a year and it promised to be a much better adventure than the one I'd been on in L.A. Actually that had stopped being an adventure after the first year and become an endless dreary existence of standing in line for auditions that never worked out. Another good reason to promise no more than a year and keep options open.

First things first. I emptied my bladder. Wouldn't want to interrupt rituals for a pee break.

Black suit. White shirt with classic dress staved collar. Black tie. Black ostrich cowboy boots. Nice touch. I'd never worn cowboy boots before. They were surprisingly comfortable. And everything was a perfect fit.

I ran a hand through my hair. Damn. Ravish was going to take one look and be glad I was the one she was taking home tonight.

I opened the door and stepped back into the study. Raider whistled.

"You clean up nice, Will."

He reopened the black hanging bag and withdrew the hooded robe. It was a kind of charcoal gray color, made of some kind of fabric that looked old, homespun or something like that. It also looked hot as blazes.

"I'm not going to be very attractive dripping with sweat and red in the face."

Raider looked amused. "No worries. It's air conditioned."

I gave the robe a dubious look. "Air conditioned."

Raider raised a blonde eyebrow. "Magic."

It wasn't that I doubted the unusual things I'd seen and heard since arriving in Wimberley, but it seemed to me that the entire community was suffering from an attack of hyperbole. Perhaps it was a delusion. Who knew how much was really "magic" and how much was coincidence? I mean, anybody could get lucky with the stock market. Right?

One thing was certain. The pull I felt toward Rave was real. I'd been separated from her for a matter of hours and was feeling anxious about it.

"Get that thing on. Kellan will help you with the hood."

"Kellan will?" asked Kellan. "What's wrong with you? You're standing right next to him."

"I don't help other men get dressed." He turned away, then as an afterthought turned back with a twinkle in his sky blue eyes. "Now, if your prizes need help getting dressed…"

"Stop right there," said Kellan, then he turned to me. "Do not pay attention to this hulk. First of all, if he even thought about looking at another woman, Harmony would turn him into an icicle and hang him from a tree for birds to peck at."

Ew.

"Second, he's as devoted to her as if he was born a species that mates for life. Like swans. When he says stuff like that, it's just his old life bubbling to the surface."

"Okay," I said.

Kellan glanced at his watch, then walked over to me. He fastened the loop hook at the neck of my robe, which made it fall into place and drape, um, like magic. Then he pulled the hood over my head.

"Careful not to muss his cute little hairdo," said Raider.

Kellan gave Raider an irritated look. "Shut up. You're starting to annoy me now."

Raider laughed like that had been his goal. "I'm not trying to annoy you, Kellan. I'm trying to annoy him!"

"Well, stop it because your irritating behavior is like a shotgun spray." Kellan pulled the hood down so that I could see if I tilted my head back a little, but it would be hard to see me with my face in shadow.

"This is ridiculous," I said.

"It'll be over soon. Then your prize will be yours and this indignity will soon be forgotten." I sighed deeply. "Time to go."

We walked to the room where the ball had been, Kellan in front, Raider bringing up the rear. I focused on the floor since that was what I could see without effort.

OFFICIALLY IZZY WAS the family beagle, but Destiny thought of him as hers and Izzy thought of himself as belonging to her. Mostly. Destiny was a little concerned about leaving him alone because he'd been causing more than his share of mischief lately.

She was looking forward to the party. The annual ceremonies weren't a chore to attend. They were fun. There would be cousins and friends and a riotous good time they would all remember forever. There was no question that she was going, but there was the worry about what Izzy would do if left alone. Then she had an idea she thought brilliant.

"There's more than one way to skin a cat," she said to Izzy.

If she'd really thought about that saying, she would have been a little horrified. Witches had stopped skinning cats around the time the real Arthur united a cluster of those barbaric little kingdoms that are now England. Still, some of the language lived on.

Opening her closet, she fetched the step stool, opened it and climbed up to reach her pink rolling Izzy-size suitcase.

"Since you don't seem to be able to behave yourself, you're going to have to go to the party with me, in this suitcase. I will leave it unzipped enough for you to breathe, but you're going to have to stay quiet and still. Understand? If you're really good, I'll give you a treat every fifteen minutes."

Izzy, who had no idea what fifteen minutes meant, looked at her with baleful eyes and sighed. He whined when she put him in the suitcase, but quietened when she gave him a T-bonz treat.

"Shhh. Be good and you'll get a bunch of those."

Her parents were curious as to why she was bringing a pink suitcase. So she lied.

"Just stuff I want to show Roslyn and Temerity."

She lifted the bag into the backseat floor space of her parents' SUV. When the vehicle started, she reached inside the bag, gave Izzy a couple of reassuring strokes, and a dog treat. It seemed her idea would work out.

THERE WERE LOTS of tables set around the perimeter of the room and more in an adjoining room. It seemed they needed even more space to accommodate the guests. No expense had been spared. Each table featured a gorgeous floral centerpiece that was unique, but still part of the theme incorporating the same flowers, greenery, and ribbons. Each table was also laden with ornate china, crystal that picked up the smallest light, and silver that looked heavy enough to belong at Buckingham Palace.

Guests were dressed in semiformal wear, men in suits, women in cocktail dresses. The prepubescent girls wore frilly party dresses. There were no boys, which seemed odd, but I supposed Rave was telling the truth about witches conceiving girls.

Two tables occupied the space in the center of the

room, each displaying a leather-bound book, a candle, a candle snuffer, and a bell. There was so much space left around them that they couldn't help but command attention. And they would even if each one didn't have a spotlight shining down on it.

The room was brightly lit with all the chandeliers and sconces on full wattage.

I looked around to see if I could spot Rave. Of course I wouldn't know which one she was. That thought caused a momentary panic, that I could be giving vows to somebody I didn't know. Then I remembered that, even if her face was hidden, I'd still recognize her voice. Anywhere.

"Wait here," said Kellan.

I was standing in a corner with another hooded figure I presumed to be Cairn Connelly and the man who spoke for him at the dinner.

"You're going first."

"Yeah," he said, voice a little shaky.

"Don't be nervous. It will be over soon and then you'll be alone with your prize. What's her name again?"

I could see just enough of his face to know that made him smile. "Deli."

"Do you know her specialty? Her, uh, magic specialty?"

"Yes." He smiled again. "She can make it rain. Anywhere. It's amazing."

I started to respond, but I felt a tug on my robe. Looking down I saw that it was Destiny wearing a big, beautiful grin. "Hi, again."

"Destiny. Hi. What's in the suitcase?"

She motioned for me to bend down then whispered, "Don't ask."

I straightened, nodded, and said, "Okay. I like your dress."

"This old thing?" she said. "My sister looks beautiful tonight. You're gonna like *her* dress."

"No way. Not Ravish. She's the ugliest girl I ever saw!"

Destiny giggled loudly, but stopped abruptly when the lights went down. "See ya."

She walked away quickly pulling her little pink bag and looking cute as a little girl could be.

Turning my attention to matters at hand, I lowered my voice and said to Cairn, "Good luck, man."

"Same to you," he replied. "Here goes nothing."

As Cairn and his prize came together in front of their bell, book, and candle, they were two indistinct figures obscured by hooded robes and could have been anyone. The spotlights on the two tables were prominent with all the other lights dimmed.

Guests had left their tables and drawn close to the center forming a tight, crowded circle.

Fortunately, they left enough space so that I could witness the proceedings. A female official in a robe that matched the couple's stood on the other side of the table and instructed them to sign their names on the first page of the book. Her hood was back so that I could see she was an attractive fiftyish woman.

Surprisingly enough, they were each asked to repeat only one vow.

"For a year and a day, we vow to cleave only unto each

other, honor our community, and keep its secrets buried deep in our hearts."

Deli took the candle snuffer and put out the flame. Cairn rang the bell.

I jumped a little when everyone broke into cheering and applause. It was such a contrast to the quiet and solemnity of the ritual, but at least I knew what to expect.

The couple removed their robes. He wore a suit similar in color to the one I was wearing, but the cut was slightly different. She wore a white cocktail dress that fell to just shy of her knees. If appearances counted for anything, they'd be solid because there was no doubt they were a beautiful couple. Judging by the way they looked at each other, they also believed they were halfway in love.

They left the ballroom with people cheering until they were out of sight.

"Your turn," Raider said from behind, giving me a slight nudge to the back. Slight in Raider's terms meant that I lurched forward.

Funny how you think of strange things at strange times. It was in that moment that I realized that I *wasn't* hot under all those clothes. Huh. Since I wasn't prepared to put stock in the notion of magically vented robes, I concluded that they probably planted a hypnotic suggestion that my body would control its temperature.

I walked forward, the hood either covering my face or leaving it in shadow. When Ravish reached my side, she took my hands in both of hers. I didn't need to hear her voice to know that the robed figure in front of me was my prize. I was already so in tune with her energy that I knew she was mine by touch.

We signed the book and repeated the vow just as the first couple had. It was at that point when madness ensued.

It would appear that one of the little girls, wandering around the house because that was more fun than the party, had discovered Glory's cat in his carrier in its usual dark and cozy spot under the kitchen island between cupboards. Naturally, the child opened the carrier and released the cat.

Just as naturally, the cat trotted toward the ballroom to appease his curiosity and see what was going on. He entered the room unseen, saw the crowd and took a turn toward the open door and adjoining room, where the kids' tables were set. That's when he smelled it. Dog.

Glory had not neutered her cat. So he met the indignation of canine on his premises with all the considerable indignation a tomcat would muster.

Destiny had left her bag underneath the table at her spot in the kids' room to join the crowd. When Izzy smelled cat, he stuck his nose through the zipper opening to get a better look at what was happening. When the beagle's head popped out of the bag, the cat was infuriated to learn that he'd been confined while a dog had stowed away with a guest and been brought into his house. He arched his back and let out a long, malicious hiss.

That act of aggression was simply too much for poor Izzy. Without the ability to exercise self-restraint, he immediately shifted into a black bear, simultaneously obliterating the once-cute pink bag, and answering the cat's hiss with a roar that could be heard for miles.

I heard someone near us ask, "What was that?" just before the crowd parted before the black bear like the Red Sea.

Understanding the smarter part of valor, Rambo ran straight for us with the bear in pursuit. Pulling Ravish well out of the path of Izzy's alter ego, I watched as the cat jumped up to the first couple's table then leapt to ours, knocking the candle over, which put it out. The bear followed close behind, stepping on the table cover which dumped everything on the floor, ringing the bell in the process. He was followed by Destiny, yelling at Izzy to stop.

I pushed my hood back then did the same for Ravish. "The candle's been snuffed and the bell has been rung. So far as I'm concerned, it's a done deal."

Rave laughed then shimmied out of her robe revealing a white, low cut, beaded version of what it takes to gobsmack a fella like me.

Following her lead, I got out of the robe and draped it over the nearest chair. "Let's get out of here," I whispered in her ear taking her hand and pulling her toward the door.

She nodded enthusiastically. "The car's out front."

"I'll drive." We ran toward the front door, hand in hand, until I stopped us. "Hold on. The ceremony has to be sealed with a kiss."

In the hallway between Kellan's study and the 'morn-ing room', I pushed Rave against the wall and proceeded to let her kiss me stupid. I knew it was dumb because my hard-on was bigger than the pants, but that's what zippers are for.

As soon as I was behind the Boxster's steering wheel, I said, "There's nobody at our house tonight, right?" She nodded. "Okay, then." I unzipped to give my cock room to breathe. I never would have guessed the sight of my engorged penis would be such a turn on for Rave. She stared like she'd never seen male parts before.

"Rave. You alright?"

"You know the way home?" she asked.

"Yeah. I think so."

"Drive."

I hit the accelerator but almost wrecked us when she bent over and took the head of my cock in her mouth. I wasn't sure if I'd just gone to heaven because Ravish was giving me a partial blowjob or if I'd gone to hell because I had to concentrate on driving.

"Rave. Goddamnit. Can you wait?"

She let my dick go with a pop. "You started it."

So that's how it was going to be. "Just till we get home. Just wait until we get home. Then I'm all yours."

"Promise?" She licked her lips which, again, almost had me running off the road.

"Promise. Stay on your side of the car for one more minute. Then I will fuck you into next Tuesday."

She treated me to her fabulous whore's laugh and made me even harder. "Holding you to that."

I didn't want to bother with the garage so I parked right in front. When the car stopped, she rushed out of the passenger side and up the steps to the porch before I could even turn off the ignition.

Running in after her I started to lock the front door.

"There's no need," she said. "No one can come in without my permission, but if it makes you feel better, go ahead turn the lock."

My hand went from the lock to her waist. If she wanted me to trust her on this, then that's what she was going to get. I pulled her in tight, my lips targeting hers like a heat-seeking missile, but she ducked away.

"Let's go upstairs. I don't want the first time to be on the floor, or the stairs, or against a wall."

"Okay," I panted, trying to stuff my dick back into my pants. "You've got a one minute head start."

I heard a tiny shriek of delight before she kicked off her high heels and ran for the stairs. Every impulse to chase was ignited by watching her run away, but I hung back for the full minute promised and used the time to undo my tie and the top button of my shirt.

Not knowing if she could hear me, I sang, "Time's up."

I pulled a pink rose out of the arrangement in the foyer and began to climb the stairs slowly. At the top of the stairs, I sang, "Almost there. Ready or not."

When I stepped inside the master suite, I could see candlelight flickering in the master bedroom. Wow. She'd been busy.

The master bedroom was indeed outfitted with what might have been a hundred white candles. It was, well, magical. But not nearly as magical as the sight of Ravish. She was standing on top of the mattress, hair let down around her shoulders, wearing nothing but a white sheet modestly wrapped around her body in the style of ancient Mesopotamians. I mentioned that I liked social studies in school, right?

I licked my lips, wanting nothing more than to grab the sheet and fall on her like a crazed animal. Apparently she liked what she saw on my face because she smiled with distinct approval. I stalked toward the bed, handed her the pink rose, and pulled her forward toward the edge of the mattress.

"Rave," I said. A hundred thoughts swirled through my mind, but the only thing that came out of my mouth was her name.

Perched on the mattress she had a height advantage of about twelve inches. She bent her head and kissed me tenderly. When she pulled back, I urged her to loosen her hold on the sheet. The fact that she resisted made me smile and made the experience of tugging on the sheet excruciatingly delicious.

"Let me see, Ravish," I said. And that was when I learned that I hold a strange power over my prize. I could see by the look on her face that she would do anything I demanded.

The knowledge that I held that power was potent enough to give me an erection that was porn-worthy. But that was nothing compared to what I felt when I pulled the sheet away from her body.

Some women might be surprised to know that men have fantasies, too. We imagine that there is one female in all creation, someone we've never seen, who is simply perfection in every possible way. Seeing Rave standing before me naked for the first time was exactly how dumb shepherds must have felt when Venus appeared to them in the altogether.

"Jesus Fucking Christ." That was the best I could manage as I stared at her breasts.

She smiled seductively as she began unbuttoning my shirt the rest of the way. I ran my hands down her sides, memorizing her body as I reveled in the touch of velvet skin.

I'll never know where the question came from, but I heard myself ask, "Am I yours?"

She grinned and nipped at my earlobe. "Let's see."

All of a sudden I was anxious about what she might think of me. I mean, I knew I had it going on, but I needed Rave to think she'd won her own prize.

She stepped off the end of the bed, shoved my suit coat off my shoulders, pulled the unbuttoned shirt free, and let it drop on the floor by the coat.

She ran her hands over my bare chest and flicked her tongue at my left nipple. I almost came right then.

The belt buckle was too close to the evidence of my arousal and I was beginning to think there could be a significant danger of being as excitable as a fourteen-year-old.

Mother of God.

I did not want to embarrass myself in front of my prize on our first turn around the block. I pulled her hands away thinking that I might calm down a little if I took off my boots. I sat down on the end of the bed. Seeing what I was doing, Rave grasped one boot and tugged. When it came free, it made her tits jiggle in the most delightful way. That did *not* help me calm down. She repeated the process for the other boot with me watching her breasts like they were going to deliver breaking news.

"Stand up," she said.

My eyes jerked to hers and locked there as I obeyed her command. She tugged my belt buckle free then pushed my pants and boxers down to my ankles. As she rose, I stepped out of the discarded clothes. She hesitated midrise when she was eye level with my cock. As she returned to a standing position she grabbed for me, enclosing as much as she could in her soft hand. When she gave it a squeeze, I gasped.

I wanted to throw her onto the bed behind her, but was temporarily paralyzed with pleasure. All I could manage was to say, "Kiss me."

You have to understand that Ravish's kisses are not just kisses. Each one is a drug that induces a more heightened state of horniness. The second she released my cock, I pushed her backward onto the bed.

Falling over her, I put my arm under her body, around her waist, and pulled her up so that we both had full use of the mattress from head to toe. When I nuzzled her neck, she gasped. I couldn't help the smile that broke out on learning that she was as easily stimulated. She moaned long and low as I rolled and tweaked the nipple of one perfectly round breast before taking it into my mouth.

Her hands were running over my back. When she began to massage my butt cheeks my pelvis involuntarily rocked forward and I groaned.

I moved my hand down to her pussy. "I'm glad you're not bare."

"Bare?" She seemed to be confused. "Oh. There. No. There's a reason why nature gave us that and one of the reasons is that the hair follicles create extra sen…"

She cried out when my hand slipped gently over her core. I slid a finger deep into the wetness.

"That's good," she said. "But I don't want your finger. I want you, Will."

"You mean my cock?"

"Yes."

"No can do, sweetheart. I'm so worked up I'm going to go off like a firecracker the minute I get inside you. Let me take care of you first."

"Don't worry about that." She pushed against my hand. "Just do it. It's what I want."

Well, the point of delayed gratification wasn't to stand on principle. It was to please my prize. She'd asked for a two-thrust come even if it meant that she was more a spectator than a participant. I figured I could make it up to her later.

So I positioned myself at her center as she encircled my waist with shapely legs and pushed in. She was so wet there was no resistance even though the size of my dick was enough to give some women pause. And there it was. Heaven to the hilt. But the strangest thing happened; I didn't explode on contact, as predicted.

I pulled out slow and raised my head so I could see her face. The emerald green of her eyes glittered with reflected candlelight. Mesmerizing.

"Look at me," she whispered.

"I am."

I pushed back in and realized that what I was feeling was the opposite of being out of control. My body was taking direction from my mind, movements controlled and gauged to maximize the experience for both of us.

"Rave," I said in a voice too deep and gravelly to be my own, "we fit perfectly."

She grinned. "Told you we were made for each other."

I made love to her slowly and deliberately for longer than I would have believed possible. When the moment felt right to move faster, she responded with a few encouraging moves of her own and, in the end, we actually experienced that elusive, practically fictitious event, the simultaneous orgasm.

Christ. Good doesn't begin to describe it. Sex with Ravish wasn't just sex. It was a transcendent experience.

It was so good that, over the next twelve hours, we experimented with six different positions in six different places: the bath, the kitchen, my study, her closet, the cabana, and the swimming pool. We sat at the kitchen island in white robes feeding fruit and cheese to each other in between sips of Zinfandel wine from their own vineyard in Fredericksburg.

Her eyes flicked to the LED clock on the microwave. "Staff will be arriving in twenty minutes."

"Nooooooo." I shook my head in denial. I wanted to stretch the moment into infinity, live there, and never leave.

"You know what they say, all things must pass."

"Let's be in denial together."

She laughed softly. "I'll go anywhere with you, Will. Even denial."

She was so perfectly mussed, disheveled hair falling around her face and shoulder in random waves, lips swollen from my kisses, and wearing such a glow I would have sworn I could see auras. At least hers.

"No. We don't need an alternate reality. The real world is looking pretty good to me right now."

Sliding off her stool, she put her arms around me for a quick hug and a big smooch on the cheek. "Quick. What do you want to do today?"

"Let's get a canoe up river, just the two of us, and float down to the taco stand for lunch."

She laughed. "Will! That's a perfect day!"

"No, it's not. A perfect day would be that followed by lots of fucking in our very fabulous bed."

With a snigger and what might have been a blush, she said, "You're the best day planner ever."

WE ENJOYED A honeymoon in the sense that, for a week or so, we did nothing but plan activities around sex. We were into each other and nothing else really mattered.

When Rave was called to her parents' house to put a no-shift spell on the beagle, it seemed she had several other magical specialties, I went with her and got to know them better. They were unquestionably accepting of me, which laid the groundwork for a really comfortable relationship.

They apologized for the way our ceremony ended and

punctuated that with a glare aimed in Destiny's direction.

I chuckled and said, "I wouldn't change it for the world. Not everybody gets their candle put out by a cat and their bell rung by a bear. It was marvelous!"

The entire family looked at me like I should be presented with the keys to the kingdom.

Rave and I went to San Antonio for a long weekend and stayed in the Presidential Suite at the Omni La Mansion Del Rio, which was right on the Riverwalk. She gave me a tour of her favorite historical sights, restaurants, and shopping.

A couple of weeks later we did the same thing in Austin, again staying in the Presidential Suite just a block away from 6th Street. She showed me the capitol, walked me all over the University of Texas campus, and introduced me to the delights of 6th Street music.

It was a whirlwind of new experiences. Believe it or not, adjusting to a super-rich lifestyle is not as easy as you might think. Not that I'm complaining. I'm just saying that it's strange to know you can have anything you want when you want it.

What I found I wanted more than any*thing* was Rave.

ONE MORNING OVER coffee on the terrace, she got around to asking what I wanted to do... other than her.

I said, "You mentioned going back to school? An ad hoc degree plan concentrating on paranormal studies?"

"Yes."

"Well, now that I know my way around campus, more or less, I think that if I could get in starting in January, that would be awesome. I don't even mind that I'll be an old man by undergraduate standards."

She scoffed. "I'm going to have to put an ugly spell on you to keep the girls off."

I laughed. "An ugly spell, huh? Don't do it. It could affect my grades."

"What?"

"Everybody is influenced by looks, Rave. At least give me a fighting chance and put an average-looks spell on me. But you don't have to worry about me being interested in what anybody else has to offer. Right?"

"Yes. I know. I just thought I'd spare UT a few hundred broken hearts."

"You're very good for my ego. You know that?"

"You have every right to a nice plump ego, Will."

SO BEGINNING IN January, I commuted to school in Austin four days a week. It was a joy because I did it in the Porsche and, if there was any question about whether or not I was flying on the wings of magic, I scored a miraculously impossible faculty parking spot right on campus.

Rave. Gotta love her.

She had offered to get me any kind of car I wanted, but there simply wasn't any car that felt more 'me' than the Boxster. I'm not saying it didn't get looks when I pulled up to my parking spot, but I was so much older than your typical undergraduate, nobody questioned it.

At the house, my study was updated with the latest tech marvels and life was paradise. I had the time to study what I loved when I wasn't in bed with Rave, which was a lot of the time. Time spent with her never got old or boring.

When I refused to shop for clothes, my closet began filling up with or without my participation. It probably won't surprise you to learn that Rave's taste in men's clothes was pretty damn good. I don't think there was a thing I didn't like, but my uniform consisted of faded jeans, faded tee shirts and handmade to-die-for cowboy boots that probably cost as much as the car. After learning how much I liked them, she filled my closet shelves with ten pairs in every shade and skin imaginable. She called it a birthday present, but the real present was her popping out of a cake as I'd requested.

I found that university, part deux, was a thing altogether different. I was focused. I was glad to be there. And the high grades that had eluded me before seemed almost effortless the second time around. When summer came, I was enjoying school too much to stay away. So I signed up for summer compression classes. Different, but also fun.

Little by little I learned the names of the people in the witch colony. And gradually I noticed that other people began calling my prize Rave instead of Ravish, which pleased me in indescribable ways.

It took months, but Raider eventually talked me into learning to ride a motorcycle. It was terrifying, but I did it. I accused my prize of putting a you-will-not-crash spell on me, but was secretly okay with it if she did.

Kellan introduced me to an old guy named Cravitt who was a metaphysical scholar. It turned out that there were a lot of intersections between the paranormal and the metaphysical. So I enjoyed spending time with him and soaking in his experience.

Rave was fun, intelligent and witty. She knew when to talk and when to let silence speak for itself. She liked the same music and TV shows. It was as good as life gets and I was so fully in the moment, I never felt the end of year creeping closer every day.

Of course everybody in the witch colony who had been there for a while was accustomed to extraordinary events. They were so commonplace that they ceased to be remarkable, but for me, I never lost a sense of wonder about it all.

For instance, one day I told Rave that the sun was blinding in my shower, coming through the east window in the mornings and asked if I could get some glass tinting or something of the sort. When I returned from school a few hours later, I found that there were no longer any east-facing windows in my bathroom, but much larger north-facing windows instead. I found her in the kitchen making a baloney sandwich.

"We could have just gotten shades for the windows in the bathroom."

"Why do things half way?" She smiled, as she offered half her sandwich to me.

I ate it out of her hand then started nibbling on her fingers while she giggled like a tween.

"One of these days will you explain how you do these things?"

"Will, when you get hungry, you look for food, eat it, and your body processes it into energy. Can you explain that?"

"Sort of."

"Liar. You cannot."

"I don't think magically replacing windows and eating food are comparable."

"That's only because you weren't born with the ability to replace windows. If you had been, you might find explaining it difficult."

"I'm gonna let that ride for now." And I did. What difference did the 'how' really make?

ANOTHER TIME, WHEN I was hiking with her in the hills, she stopped me and indicated that I should be still. She quietly pulled out field glasses, handed them to me and pointed to a location slightly above and to the northwest of us.

Bringing the glasses to my eyes, I adjusted the focus and began panning to see what was of interest. When I came to the huge mountain lion sunning itself on a flat rock, I know I jumped. The thing was beautiful, magnificent even. It was also terrifying.

Rave whispered, "Time to go," then the cat disappeared. One second it was there. Then it wasn't. That also made me jump.

"What the hell?" I lowered the glasses and looked at Rave accusingly.

"He doesn't belong here. Too many people. I sent him to Big Bend where he'll be more at home."

"You sent him? You mean you teleported that huge beast nearly five hundred miles?"

She shrugged, sniffed, and turned away as she began walking back down the trail. "Call it what you want. I poofed him. He was here. Now he's there."

"And he's unharmed?" I hurried after her.

She stopped abruptly and looked a little incensed. "Of course he's unharmed. What do you take me for?"

"A creature who wields staggering power."

"And you think I'd misuse it?"

There was no question that she was indignant and no question that I was out of line simply because I was out of my purely human depth. "I'm not saying that. Exactly."

"We work hard at making sure that nobody abuses their gifts, Will. Anytime you think that of me, feel free to take it to the Council and they'll begin an inquiry."

That was new. "The Council?"

"Let's go home. Have a bath and dinner."

"No. Wait. What about the Council? Who are they and what do they do?"

She sighed. "Tell you on the drive home."

I was temporarily appeased, but as soon as we were in the Jeep and on the highway, I started in again like a dog after a bone.

"Council, Rave."

"It's a self-governing body set up to insure that the very thing that's spooking you doesn't happen. My mother currently serves. If we're going to live in close proximity to the general population, we have to be sure that our special talents remain in check."

"What was the catalyst?"

"Sometimes you're too smart, Will."

"Not an answer, Rave."

"Okay. Okay. It was over a hundred years ago. There was a dispute between the colony and the mayor of Wimberley. One of us decided to resolve the dispute in ways that were severely unpleasant for the mayor and his family. She punctuated that with a vague threat that it would be imprudent for any future city government official to oppose the will of the colony.

"Naturally the whole thing made people afraid of us. And we can't have that. When people are afraid, torches and pitchforks usually follow. Not that torches and pitchforks are a threat to us, but you know, it gets messy. So the colony elders got together and decided on a punishment of banishing, which really is the worst thing imaginable for one of us. They decided that having a regulatory body was a good idea and turned it into a pillar of the community.

"The Council renews perpetually with a constant seven members who are above reproach. If anyone is suspected of doing anything that might create problems for the colony, they're given a fair hearing and then they're given the boot."

"I see."

"The reality is that purely human residents of Wimberley enjoy all kinds of benefits because of our presence that they wouldn't have otherwise."

Purely human?

"Like what?"

"Like super clean drinking water. Just the right amount of rainfall, not too much, not too little. Price control on rents and groceries. Financial support for the schools and hospitals. They're the best to be found anywhere. Stuff like that. Nobody in Wimberley lives in a cardboard box under a bridge."

I thought back to the two old codgers who were on the porch of the hotel the day I met Destiny. One of them had said, "She's one of them." They'd been amused by my reaction to Izzy's performance, but they were clearly not afraid. In fact, it was almost said affectionately, like they think of witches as patron saints.

"You think the townspeople know what you are and like having you here?"

"Some know. The rest suspect. Do they like what we do for the town?" She grinned. "Of course. They're not stupid."

"I didn't mean to insult you when I asked if the disappeared cat was okay."

She pursed her lips and stared at the road. "How are you going to make it up to me?" Slanting her eyes sideways, she gave me the smile I'd come to know as an indicator that she was in the mood for a good licking.

"I'll buy you chili cheese fries at the tavern."

"What else?"

"I'll run you a nice warm bath."

"What else?"

"I'll eat you until you scream my name thirteen times."

That got me a grin. "And then you shall be forgiven."

ChAPTER EiGHT

D AYS, WEEKS, AND months flew by. It was a little strange, studying the paranormal from an academic and historical standpoint, while living in the middle of a colony of witches. But it was also a very fine secret to have.

I enjoyed my classes, but found that I couldn't wait to get back to Rave. Not that I had to be with her every minute. I spent a lot of time in my study, but knowing she was in the house, or would be soon, was a comfort.

I remembered that her birthday was October fourteenth and wanted to do something special. So I'd asked Kellan and Glory if we could have a party at their place then asked Simon to help me with a special musical tribute. What I had in mind was right up his alley, so he was glad to help.

Rave's mother, Chalice, did most of the planning and somehow managed to keep it a secret. I'd told my prize that we were invited to dinner at Kellan's and asked her to wear the red dress she'd worn the first time I'd seen her at the ball. I made no mention of her birthday, wanting her to believe that I didn't remember.

"Are you sure?" she asked. "Seems like overdressing. Glory is likely to be wearing Daisy Dukes."

"No. Kellan said dress up and I told him we would."

She accepted that explanation. Thank goodness.

I pulled out the suit I'd worn to our bell, book, and candle ceremony. It fit perfectly.

"Rave!" I called, going to the door to my bathroom.

"Yes!" she answered from inside her bath.

"Did you put a stay-the-same-size spell on me?"

"Yeah. I told you I was going to."

I looked in the mirror and smiled. I'd spent months eating with abandon, but kept my figure. How could I object to that?

We stepped into the bedroom at the same time.

"Still the most beautiful creature alive," I said and meant every word.

She grinned like it was the first time she'd ever been told that she was a goddess walking.

I TEXTED CHALICE to let her know we were leaving. Everybody in the colony had either walked to Kellan's or been shuttled there by golf cart so that there wouldn't be any extra cars or valet parkers to tip Rave off.

We pulled up to the front door, climbed the steps and rang the bell. The butler answered.

"Good evening, Mr. Draiocht, Ms. Wimberley."

"Hello, Roberto."

He closed the front door and said, "Right this way."

We followed him along the familiar way to the ballroom.

"They're having us for dinner in the ballroom?" Rave asked.

"Maybe," I said noncommittally, hoping she didn't pick up any hesitancy in my answer.

When Roberto opened the large double doors the entire colony shouted, "SURPRISE!"

She was indeed surprised. She flushed a beautiful pink in her cheeks and laughed her deep throaty laugh.

"You devil!" she said to me and I took that as high praise.

According to Chalice's instructions all the women and girls wore white, all the men wore black suits like mine. Only Rave was in red so that she stood out like the star that she was in my mind.

I leaned over and nuzzled her ear. "Happy Birthday."

We ate her favorite things and drank her favorite cocktails while people took the mic, one after another, to tell stories about Rave growing up. In between, a live band, made up of colony residents, played soft pop hits and gave the occasion a festive ambiance.

I'd planned to give her my present between dinner and dessert and was getting more nervous by the minute. I'm sure she saw the nerves because she said, "Is something wrong?"

"No. I'll be back in a minute." I excused myself, nodding at Rave's family, who were sitting at our table.

Simon was sitting across the room. I gave him a signal when I got his attention. He rose and made his way to the head of the room along with me. When I took the mic, he was handed an electric guitar by one of the musicians.

"Hey, everybody," I said, trying not to sound nervous. "Thank you all for coming to help us celebrate Rave's birthday. This may have been my idea, but the entire credit for putting on this bash goes to Chalice. I'd still be trying to figure out where to start if not for her.

"Anyway, Simon has helped me with a little something special that I have to say."

I'd never sung in public before and was half petrified, but the other half was determined. I knew I wanted to do a cover version of Buddy Holly's classic *Rave On* and when I started trying to decide how to do it, I discovered it had been covered about a hundred times in widely diverse ways. In the end, Simon and I decided on the Rolling Stones version. Thankfully it was a short song. That's what I kept telling myself.

Right on cue, somebody brought a chair and placed it on the floor right in front of where I stood on the raised platform.

"Rave," I said. "You're needed down here. Front and center."

She looked around like she was unsure and for a minute I thought she might refuse, but with applause and encouragement, she managed to make her way toward me and sit in the chair. I'd say her look was a mixture of curiosity, anticipation, and glare.

It didn't take long for her to get into the spirit of things once the music started and I wish I had a still shot of her face when I started to sing, "I'm gonna tell you how it's gonna be. You're gonna give your love to me."

People got up and began dancing all around Rave. By the end of the song she was looking at me like I'd handed her the moon. Just what I was going for.

At midnight I took her home. I'd had the bedroom outfitted with a hundred white candles, as it had been the first night we'd been together. A bottle of sweet red wine was on ice, just the way she liked it. Yes. I know wine connoisseurs everywhere who are managing to not cringe about the idea of sweet red are having apoplexy thinking about red wine on ice. But Rave was entitled to her preferences, especially on her birthday.

I made love to her exquisitely slowly, playing her body like an instrument, using every detail I'd learned about how to send her into a state of ecstasy.

Afterward, I snuffed out the candles, came back to bed and lay on my back while she snuggled into her favorite cuddle position.

"How are we ever going to plan a one year party to top that?" she said in the darkness.

"One year party?"

"Yes. It's coming up. Our year and a day is on All Hallows, October thirty-first. That's just… seventeen days from now."

Perhaps my heart didn't speed up as much as I thought because, after a few minutes, I heard her breathing even out. I'd been living in denial about the built-in expiration date on the good life, but my avoidance tactic had just hit a wall.

Confrontation dead ahead.

I stared at the ceiling, knowing I only had just a little over two weeks left with the woman sleeping on my chest. I remember thinking it was a shame that I didn't believe in love because, if I did, I would surely be head over heels in love with my Rave.

After a couple of hours of staring at the ceiling, I eased myself out from under her. She hummed a little, but let me go and went back to sleep.

After pulling on a pair of sweatpants, I padded downstairs. No shirt. No shoes. Neither was needed. The temperature in the house was always perfect. I poured myself an inch of whiskey from the good stash, took it to my study, sat down at my desk and looked around.

King of all I survey.

Two weeks.

That's all I had left.

Two measly little weeks. I knew they'd go by so fast they were already gone.

I knew I had to start figuring out how and when to tell Rave. I'd been honest up front. I'd told her that I didn't believe in love, certainly didn't believe in forever, and that I was promising a year and no more. She'd said okay, but tonight, when she mentioned the one year party... It was clear she thought I'd changed my mind.

As I sat there, nursing a scotch, I could feel my anger toward her start building. She was making me feel guilty about leaving and she had no right to do that. I never promised more than I had to give. Still, I needed to figure out a way to let her down easy.

I needed a plan for when and how to tell her. There was no question about the fact that I couldn't let her start planning a party. That would be as bad as being left standing at a wedding altar. And even if I was mad at her for forgetting I'd only promised a year, I didn't want to see her hurt like that.

Decision made.

When she said something about starting party planning, I would tell her. Christ. It was never supposed to be so complicated.

That was the first time I saw Deck Durbin's ghost. He materialized on one of the leather sofas wearing the garb and accoutrements of a Texas Ranger.

I froze, every bit as shocked as I imagined an absolute skeptic would be.

He turned his head my direction and simply said, "No."

I don't think his voice was audible. His mouth moved and I heard the word in my head, but I don't think there was actual sound. Pulling myself together, I was just about to ask what the devil he meant by, "No," when he disappeared.

Even though I had hoped to see the highwayman's ghost sometime during my year in Wimberley, I was unprepared for a personal visit and especially not in my personal sanctuary. It felt a little like my life had been breached and I resented it.

"So you want the last word, huh?" I said to thin air. "Well, you had the first, last, and only word, but you suck at communicating!"

I stared at the sofa for several minutes thinking he might have a response, but I remained the sole occupant of the room, corporeal or otherwise.

Seventeen days. That's what was left of my year in paradise. I wasn't going to be thrown out of the Garden of

Eden. I was going to walk out on my own. Part of me thought that made me both idiot and ass. But the part making the decision couldn't stand feeling caged. And a priceless museum-quality rococo cage is still a cage.

It was simple. If the door was open, I'd stay indefinitely. Indefinitely might turn into forever. Who could say? But the idea of permanent, can't-be-undone, commitment scared the shit out of me.

Having reached my decision, I set the glass in the kitchen sink, climbed the stairs and crawled back into bed. Rave turned toward me and nestled into my side like she belonged there. Imagining sleeping alone, when I'd become so accustomed to the feel of Rave in my bed, made my heart hurt a little, but I couldn't pay attention to such things. Those thoughts were threads that could form the net that would trap me.

Seventeen days.

I turned toward Rave and inhaled the scent of her cedar and dragonsblood shampoo. As I finally drifted off, I was thinking I'd miss that.

Chapter nine

I HAD A four day reprieve in the sense that I didn't have to tell Rave outright that I was leaving at the end of my contract. It wasn't a carefree four days because she kept asking me what was wrong. Jesus. No wonder I never got an acting job. I sucked at acting.

On the fifth day we went down into town for greasy burgers and greasier fries.

"Harmony wants to host our one-year party. We don't have to have everybody like last time. We could ask just a few people if you want. Also, you had said something about going to see your family. We could do that right after if you want. Take the trip we talked about. Go through New Orleans. Drive along the coast. Stop at the Hard Rock in Biloxi and gamble a little. What do you think?"

What did I think?

I thought that sounded like heaven. I had to beat back an image of driving along the shore at Pass Christian with the Boxster's top down, Rave's hair blowing in the breeze. I'd have to be a fool to turn that down, a fool or some guy who was so paranoid about being boxed in that he was willing to give up everything for freedom.

What was that line from Bobby Mcgee? *Freedom's just another word for nothing left to lose.*

Bottom line was that I was more afraid of closing all the doors on all the possibilities life had to offer than I was of living without Rave.

Looking down at her burger basket, I could see that she was almost finished.

"Come on," I said. "I have something to tell you and I don't want to talk about it in here."

A line formed between her brows, but she said, "Okay."

That was Rave. She was agreeable unless something was a ten with her.

We walked out to the parking lot in silence. When we'd closed the doors to the Jeep, she said, "What is it?"

I looked over at her, sitting behind the wheel. So beautiful. I didn't want to tell her, but I didn't want to lead her on and leave like a thief in the night either. She deserved better. She deserved to be told straight up.

"I promised a year. And a year is all I have to give." Her lips parted and I heard a tiny gasp. Her eyes were wide, searching mine, and I was afraid she wasn't breathing. "Rave. I'm sorry. It's not you. You're perfect. It's just that I…"

My hand was in midair, reaching over to stroke her cheek and console her, when she slapped it away. The expression on her face changed from heartbroken to furious in the blink of an eye.

"Do not touch me. And don't call me that, either. If you've made your decision and you know you're not staying, I want you to go now."

"What? Wait a minute. I still have twelve days."

"You have what I give you. This car. Your clothes. Five thousand dollars. And no memories of ever having been here."

"But…"

"No talking, Willem. I never want to hear your voice again."

I closed my mouth and faced forward.

Rave pulled out her phone and speed dialed while she was driving.

"Hi," I heard her say. "Are you home?" Pause. "Willem won't be staying when our year is up." Pause. "Yes. He's sure." Pause. "I'm dropping him off at your house in five minutes. I'll have Ed pack his things and deliver them with the car and some traveling money. You do the rest." Pause. "Yeah. I'm fine." She ended the call and tossed the phone into the cup holder.

This was not how I thought things would go, but maybe she was right. Maybe it was better to pull the Bandaid off quick.

I said nothing as we passed the turn to our house, but it did make my heart hurt – the idea of never seeing our home again…

Rave pulled up in front of Raider's house. Staring straight ahead, she said, "Get out."

"Rave, I…"

"OUT!" she yelled, leaning over me to open the passenger door. Clearly, she wasn't kidding.

Again, this was not how I pictured this. I'd imagined a

lengthy goodbye with lingering kisses, maybe a few tears. This was not the way it was supposed to go.

I pushed the passenger door all the way open and got out. Before I closed the door, I bent down and said, "I'm sorry."

She took off without waiting for me to close the door. I stood on the driveway and watched until she disappeared around the bottom of the hill, out of sight. The door opened behind me.

"Come in, Will. We have a few things to talk about. Raider will be home shortly."

Raider. He was probably going to finish the job he started in the river the day I tipped him over.

I turned around. I'd never seen Harmony look sad and it didn't make me feel good, knowing I was the one who'd put that look on her face.

Without a word I climbed the steps and went inside. I followed her to the morning room and sat at the glass top table.

"You want something to drink?" she asked.

"Uh, no. We just ate at the tavern. I'm good."

"Well, let's get started then. First of all, you should know that you have the infamy of being the first and *only* contest winner to ever leave at the end of his one year contract."

Since there was nothing to say to that, I said nothing.

"When Ravish's man arrives with the car and your things, you'll be escorted to the gates. You have from now until the time you cross the city limits to change your mind. Once you drive past the Wimberley city limits, you will have no memory of anything that has happened since before you took the card with the contest number on it. Do you understand? Is this what you want?"

That was such a complicated question. "It's really *not* what I want, Harmony, but it's what I have to do."

"Alright then. I'll leave you alone. If you need anything to eat or drink, you know the way to the kitchen."

She left me to the silence and solitude of the morning room in the afternoon. Since the sun was overhead, it was less bright, but not less beautiful. I was thinking about all the things I would miss, when the ghost appeared, standing across the table from where I sat.

"Willem Draiocht. You shall not leave."

He 'spoke' in an accent that was English, but not like any I'd heard.

"Is that what you meant when you said, 'No', before?"

"Leaving Ravish Wimberley would be a grave error in judgment. Are you dead set on walking the hallways of hell with me?"

"I can't stay."

"You cannot leave."

He vanished after that repeated pronouncement, just as someone from the kitchen popped her head in.

"Can I bring you something while you wait, Mr. Draiocht?"

"No. Nothing. Thank you."

She hadn't been gone a full minute before I heard Raider's heavy boot stomp coming toward the morning room.

"Will! Goddamnit. What the fuck do you think you're

doing?"

He didn't look any happier than Harmony.

"I can't stay, Raider."

"Why the fuck not?"

The Voice was screaming that same question at me, over and over. "I can't live behind a locked door."

He shook his head. "What does that mean?"

"If I promise to stay in a permanent no-way-out relationship with Ravish, I might as well be a prisoner at Huntsville."

He looked at me like I was certifiable. "Huntsville? There's not a single guy in Huntsville who wouldn't do *anything* to trade places with you. Don't compare your life here to prison. That's ridiculous." He ran a hand through his hair. "What about your friends? Forget that. What about Rave? Don't you care about breaking her heart? Don't you love her?"

"Yes. I care about her and I don't like breaking her heart. But no, I don't believe in love."

"You don't believe in love." His repetition was dripping with derision. "Well, wake up, fool. It just so happens that love believes in you. That thing that you're feeling right now? The pull that says you'd like to kick your own ass for hurting her? That's love. When you go to Austin to take your little classes and can't wait to get back to her? That's love. When you can't imagine ever fucking another woman no matter what the circumstances? That's love.

"The way you looked at her when you sang that old song on her birthday? You wouldn't find one person who was in that room who wouldn't swear that what they were seeing was, yeah, you guessed it. Love."

That was probably more words than Raider had spoken in a week, but I just sat there shaking my head.

He raised his arms and let them fall to his sides. "You're really going through with it," he said, beginning to resign himself to the fact that I couldn't be talked out of it. He pulled out a chair and slumped into it. "You know it's permanent. You can't change your mind later. If you leave, you're gone for good. There's no way back."

That made my heart beat faster. I hated the idea of no way back. That was another kind of permanent that was unappealing, but I'd made up my mind. "I know," I whispered.

Raider sat without speaking for half an hour then rose and left the room without another word. Another twenty minutes after that, someone was sent to tell me that my things were waiting for me outside.

Making my way back to the front, I realized that I was sorry to not have the chance to say goodbye to Kellan and Simon and so many others I'd come to feel close to.

The Boxster was waiting with the top down and the driver's side door open. It was polished and detailed to showroom perfection.

Ed stood next to the car. "Your things are packed and in the trunk, sir."

"Thank you, Ed. For everything."

He bowed his head in acknowledgement. "Sorry to see you go, sir."

Harmony and Raider had come out onto the porch. Big tears were streaming down her face. Raider was embracing her from behind, looking both angry and grim. He probably wanted to kick my ass for making his wife cry.

"Sorry," I said and it sounded lame even to me. "Tell Ravish I said thank you for the car and… everything."

I walked around to the driver's side, but before I could slide under the wheel, Deck Durbin appeared, blocking my way.

"You will not go," he said.

"This is getting old. Get out of the way. I'm going."

"Who is he talking to?" I heard Raider ask Harmony.

I looked up in time to see her shake her head. "You don't see him?"

"See who?" she asked.

"The ghost. Deck Durbin."

"No, Will. I don't see him."

I turned back to the car. "Whether they see you is neither here nor there. Get out of the way. You're just prolonging the inevitable."

"Love is everything," he said. "I refused to accept that when I was alive and now I'm cursed to live like this. In hell. You know what hell is, Willem? It's knowing I'll never see Pleasant again. There's no second chance for me. But you can be saved! Don't go. Listen to your heart. Stop while you can."

When I reached up to shove him out of the way, he vanished.

With one last look at Raider and Harmony, I got in the car and drove away. Slowly. Reliving the memories I'd made during my year in the colony. Good memories.

Memories I wished I could treasure forever.

I knew where I was headed. Southeast to San Marcos, on to I10 which would take me all the way home to Fairhope. Twenty yards away from the city limit sign, the car stalled. Just as I was thinking that was impossible, Durbin appeared in the passenger side of my car dressed like a highwayman.

He'd become more than a supernatural curiosity. He'd evolved a first rate pest.

"Christ," I said.

"I was like you," he began. "So sure there was more. There wasn't more. When I was home with Pleasant and our girls, I held everything in my hands. I gave it away for an illusion. It was an illusion that cost me my soul. Hear me well, Willem Draiocht. You are about to surrender your own soul to a life of empty searching, trying to recapture what you already have, but failing.

"Love is the only thing worth dying over and the only thing worth living for. From this side of the veil I can see more clearly than you. For your own sake. For the last time. Do. Not. Go."

The worst part was, I think I knew deep down that he was telling the truth. But I was so stubborn, I left anyway.

CHAPTER TEN

I WAS SPEEDING east on I10 when I 'woke up'. I don't have any other way to explain it. I became aware of my surroundings when I heard a siren behind me. I looked in the rearview mirror and, sure enough, I was being pulled over. After easing to the shoulder, I turned the car off and waited.

While the patrolman was doing whatever they do, I tried to get my bearings. I was in one incredibly sweet ride although I had no idea how I got there. It wasn't my car and I hoped to heck that while I was sleepwalking, or whatever, I hadn't stolen it. But I must have stolen it. How else would I be driving it and why else would I be stopped by law enforcement?

My heartrate shot through the roof while I imagined being sent to federal prison to become designated chew toy for some beefy tattooed guy with an IQ that equaled room temperature. I was lost in the horror of that scenario, when the patrolman approached.

"Good day, sir."

"Officer," I said, hoping my voice didn't sound too shaky.

"Can I see your license and insurance?"

"Um, sure."

I leaned over to retrieve my wallet. When I opened it, I realized it contained a lot of hundred dollar bills. It also contained an Alabama driver's license showing my parents' address in Fairhope.

"Here you go." I handed him the license, then opened the glove box to look for proof of insurance, hoping to hell there wouldn't be a gun in there. Or drugs. After all, I was a high end car thief who might also be high. There was no telling what I'd done.

There were papers. One was the car registration with my name and the Fairhope address. Under that was proof of insurance, also with my name and the Fairhope address. The relief almost made me sag in my seat, knowing that however I'd come by the car, it probably wasn't dishonestly.

Handing over the insurance, I said, "What exactly is the problem, Officer?"

"You were doing eighty-seven in a seventy-five mile per hour stretch. And I'm going to have to write you a speeding ticket for that."

"Oh. Okay."

I sat quietly while he wrote out the ticket. When he was finished, he handed it to me. "You can pay by mail or show up for your court date. Your choice. Here's your license and insurance. Have a nice day."

"Yeah. You, too."

I put my license back in my wallet, threw the proof of insurance back in the glove box, and started the car. The next exit was Schulenburg. I pulled into the Whataburger conveniently located on the off ramp. Inside, I headed straight for the men's room. After closing myself in a stall, I pulled out my wallet and counted the bills. Five thousand dollars.

Looking down I saw that I was wearing faded jeans, a faded Luckenbach tee shirt, a Tag Heuer watch that looked like it was more valuable than the franchise I stood in, and cowboy boots that were not only gorgeous, but felt great on my feet.

Huh.

I decided to put a Whatachicken in my stomach while I was trying to sort out where I was and why. Maybe I had amnesia. On the way in I'd looked back at the car and noticed the license plate. Alabama. The one with the pretty blue water and sky. It was personalized and said 'GON4GUD'. Another strange piece of a truly bizarre puzzle. It did make a pretty contrast with the tomato red Boxster though.

I got the sandwich, took it to a back table, and sat down where I could keep an eye on the car. Everybody who pulled into the Whataburger slowed down to get a look at it. I guess they didn't see one of those in Schulenburg every day.

Speaking of that, where was Schulenburg? I got out my phone and pulled it up on GPS. Schulenburg was on I10 in far south Texas. Apparently I was heading east toward Houston.

Or home.

Yeah.

I must be going home.

What was the last thing I remembered?

Of course. I was quitting acting. That's why I was going home. That didn't explain the car or the memory loss, but whatever had happened, I seemed to have landed on my feet with a dream ride, five thousand dollars and damn nice boots.

As I was sliding back into the Boxster to get back on the road, a local kid yelled, "Sweet wheels."

I smiled and waved, sincerely wishing I could remember how I came to be the owner of the car.

It was just about six when I blew past the Houston city limits. Since I was going to have to stop somewhere for the night, I thought Houston would be a good choice. There wouldn't be another five star hotel before New Orleans and, for some reason, I was feeling drained. I couldn't leave a car like the Boxster in the parking lot of a Motel 6 overnight. Hell no. Nothing less than secure valet parking in a hotel with excellent insurance just in case the parking turned out not to be secure.

After pulling off the road, I pulled out my phone. It was bigger than I'd remembered and in a nicer case, but everything worked the same. I looked up five star hotels near I10. Four Seasons. I dialed the number.

"Four Seasons Houston. How may we help you?"

"Reservations."

"My pleasure."

"Reservations. How can I help you?"

"I need a room for tonight. You got something?"

"We do. Yes. But there is a large meeting taking place here and we're almost full. We'll need a credit card."

"Oh. Alright."

I didn't know if I had a credit card. I pulled my wallet out of my pants and found several cards including a black American Express. Surely I'd remember if I'd won the lottery. Right?

After reading them the number and expiration date, I put the Four Seasons address into the car's nav system and decided to put the top up because it was looking like rain. I popped the trunk. Lo and behold. In addition to the deck where the soft top was stored, there were two large and one small rolling suitcases. The luggage was leather and looked like it could easily hurt Bill Gates's travel budget. Huh.

My curiosity about what was in the bags could wait until I got to the hotel. The task at hand was getting the top on the car. Well, I'm not the most mechanical sort and the top came in two user-unfriendly pieces. Thank goodness for video instruction guides online. The car manual was practically useless, but I followed YouTube instructions and got the thing on. I wouldn't swear it was hurricane-proof, but the wind noise wasn't bad.

On the road again, I decided to turn on the radio and discovered two things. First, the car had satellite. Second, I learned that I have damn good taste in music. The dial was set to Road Trip. New music. Old music. Innovative covers. Good stuff.

At the hotel, I told the valet to have all the luggage sent to my room. The clerk looked impressed by the black American Express and smiled when I asked him to break a hundred dollar bill for tips. I wasn't sure why I felt so at home in a five star hotel. But I did.

I got on the elevator with a guy wearing a tux. He looked me up and down and said, "Nice boots."

I couldn't help but smile. "Thanks. They're my favorites."

I didn't know if that was true, but it sounded good and could be true. Hell. Maybe I was an actor after all.

The room was nice enough. I was thinking it was nothing to write home about when it hit me that I must have gotten used to a luxurious lifestyle at some point. My life was a mystery, but at least I woke up in a five star lifestyle.

When the luggage arrived, I gave the guy a nice tip.

After turning on the TV news I unzipped the first case to see what kind of stuff I'd packed for my trip home. That was when I heard the announcer say that it was the twentieth day of October, a year later than my last memory.

Jesus. I've lost a year?

How could that be possible? On the other hand, how could it be possible that I'd acquired a Porsche, luggage too good for Prince Charles, and a black American Express? Not to mention the cowboy boots.

Hold on. That meant the AX was expiring in eleven days, at the end of the month. I wondered if they'd be sending a new one to my parents' address, but my intuition doubted it. I don't know why.

After sitting down on the side of the bed to process losing a year, I looked at the news and tried to absorb what I might have missed through current events. It seemed like life had pretty much marched on with or without me.

After a few minutes I was recovered enough to want to look in the luggage again. I opened the heaviest bag first and quickly found out why it was heaviest. One entire zippered side contained cowboy boots. Six pairs. The other side contained jeans, twill pants, and shorts.

The second bag had tees and collared knit shirts neatly folded on one side, with socks, boxers, flip flops, Chucks, and a leather jacket that managed to look both expensive and cool at the same time on the other.

Whatever I'd been up to, I was a casual kind of guy.

That left the smallest case. Toiletries, a professional hair dryer, and a book about sightings of a ghost in a little town called Wimberley, Texas. The name sounded familiar.

Was that what I was doing? Paranormal research? I'd gone chasing after ghost stories? It'd be nice to know what I found out. Maybe I was one of those ghost hunter guys on TV. Or maybe I was a producer of a show, scouting around for good material. Maybe I'd just been heading home for a visit.

I pulled out my phone and went through the contacts list. All my acting contacts were there. All my bartending contacts were there. Nobody else except for family.

Messages didn't give up any clues either. No messages at all. None sent by me. None received by me.

Pressing my mother's contact number I listened to the ring.

"Hello?"

"Mom, hey."

"Will! How are you?"

"Good. I'm actually on the way there. Didn't I tell you I was coming?"

"No. I think I'd remember something as momentous as that."

I chuckled. "Okay. Well, should be there tomorrow night."

"In time for dinner?"

"If you like."

"Of course I like. I'll make your favorites."

She sounded as excited as if she'd won stuff on a game show and I wondered what I'd done to deserve great parents.

"I'll save up room and come starved."

"You do that, sugarbunch. I can't wait to see you."

It was so comforting to hear her thick Southern drawl. It had all but disappeared in modern times, what with Midwestern being spoken from a flat screen while grabbing a beer at the bar, waiting in line at the bank, waiting for a flight at the airport, even waiting for the gas tank to fill up.

"Love you. See you soon."

I ended the call and looked at the open suitcases. How was I going to explain all this?

I'd spent a lot of time sitting in the car. Maybe a walk would clear my head.

When I got down to the street, I asked the doorman, "I want to walk a little and eat a little. What do you recommend?"

"Fancy or just good food?"

"Just good food."

"You like Chipotle?"

"Who doesn't like Chipotle?"

He chuckled. "It's about eight blocks."

"That's perfect. It's a nice night."

"Yes, sir. Exactly seventy degrees."

He gave me directions. I gave him a tip.

It felt good to walk. I arrived ten minutes before they closed at eight so I ordered a burrito to go. I walked it back to Discovery Green, which was only a block from the hotel, bought a beer from a small step-in bar, and ate on a park bench while listening to a small jazz band playing for tips.

Everything about the moment was good. The burrito. The beer. The park. The music. The temperature. The fact that I had a black American Express in my pants and a Porsche Boxster parked at the Four Seasons where I was staying. So why did I feel so unsettled? So incomplete? Like something absolutely essential was missing?

It was inexplicable. I had the feeling that I was missing a chunk of my stomach, the place where peace and sense of well-being reside.

AFTER A RESTLESS night of dreaming about being arrested for auto theft, identity theft, credit card theft, and burrito theft, I checked the weather the next morning before I left. Sunny all the way. So I reverse engineered the convertible top using the same method. You Tube video. The valet parker was a big help. I found out that it's easier with two people.

I sped through east Texas, over the Atchafalaya Swamp, took I12 north of Pontchartrain because it was the most direct route, but got off long enough to find a lakefront crawfish bar for lunch.

When I got back on the road, I passed a turn off to New Orleans and felt something tug at my mind. There was something about that I was supposed to know, but couldn't remember.

I picked I10 up again close to the Mississippi border, but decided to take old Highway 90 to Biloxi because it hugged the shoreline and was a beautiful drive. I remembered that from times I'd driven the route before the L.A. years.

The water was gorgeous, the sunlight creating a sea of sparkling silver over blue. I alternated between watching the road and appreciating the scenery. Going through Pass Christian I turned my head to the right to see the beach. For a second I thought I saw a woman in the car with me, hair black as night pulled back into a ponytail that was ruffling in the breeze. I didn't see her face. It startled me enough that I jerked the wheel and got a honk from a truck in the oncoming lane.

When I felt safe enough to glance back at the passenger seat, no one was there. I was pretty sure I was going crazy.

When I passed the casinos and resort hotels at Biloxi, the Hard Rock caught my attention. What was it about that? Something I couldn't quite remember, but it bothered me like an itch that couldn't be scratched.

As planned, I made it through Mobile before rush

hour and pulled into the driveway at Fairhope right at five o'clock. By the time I got the door open and stepped out of the car, my mother was rushing out the door.

"Oh, my lands, you're a sight for sore eyes, Willem!" She pulled me down so that she could give me big smooches on both cheeks. Her enthusiasm made me laugh and temporarily forget my troubles. Eventually she was able to take adoring eyes away from me and look at the car. "And what heaven's name is this?"

"Car."

"I'll say! Looks like a nice one. Love the color. And I think it suits you. So does this mean you're a movie star?"

"Hardly. It means I'm a failed actor slinking home with his tail between his legs."

"Well, you slink in mighty fine style."

"Come get settled in while I finish dinner. What do you think we're having?"

"Fried catfish?" She nodded and grinned. "Lots of lemon slices and tartar sauce?"

"Of course. If I didn't know that about you, I wouldn't be your mama."

"Mashed potatoes?" She nodded. "Green beans with bacon?"

"Hundred percent correct. And a special surprise for dessert."

"Nobody cooks like you, Mom. It's kind of a wonder that I escaped from home without weighing three hundred pounds."

"Oh, now. We have salad sometimes."

I laughed. "Yeah. As an appetizer before an entrée of

something deep fried."

"Well, I don't cook Cal-fusion cuisine. Whatever that is."

"I could explain it."

"No."

"Okay. Is it just the three of us for dinner tonight?"

"Don't be ridiculous. Everybody is coming."

"Oh, good." I wasn't sure I sounded sincere, but I tried.

Actually I was glad there'd be a crowd because it would be easier to hide all the stuff I didn't know about my life. I hauled the bags around to my old room at the back of the house. There was something really comforting about the fact that it hadn't changed at all in ten years. Maybe the folks had left it alone because I was the only one who didn't have a *real* home.

My two older brothers had gone into the construction business with my dad and were doing well. My sister's husband worked at the resort so, strange as it is in this day and time, the entire family stayed close by in Fairhope.

That meant that the house would be filled to bursting with siblings, in-laws, nieces, nephews, and me. Mom fussed that there was no hope of seating everybody at the large dining table so we had to be satisfied with just the adults. The older kids were allowed to fill plates and eat on the picnic tables outside. The kids too young for that were fed in the kitchen, moms running back and forth between adult talk and kiddie care.

It was a circus.

And I loved it.

Right up to the minute when the dreaded question popped up.

"So, Will, what about that car?"

Geoffrey asked the question, but it could have been anybody. They all wanted to know.

I'd been over the answer to that question a hundred times in my head and still didn't have a satisfactory answer. At the moment of truth, I lied.

"It was a parting gift from my agent. I think she felt bad about the fact that she'd never gotten me a single acting job in ten years." Eight pairs of eyes stared at me like they were waiting for more. "Sorry, guys. There's no more to the story. The car looks good, but it's not new. I got it used."

"Oh, well," said Geoff. "That makes *all* the difference."

Geoff was born second after my brother, Thadeus. He liked to stir the pot, which was exactly what he was doing.

"Yeah," is all I said.

Mom rescued me. "Well, it's a beautiful car. It's nice you have something to show for the time you spent in California."

"So what are you gonna do now?" asked Thaddie.

"Go back to school. And maybe write some young adult fantasy books."

"About what?" asked my sister, Vivienne.

I smiled. "I had this idea about a beagle who thinks he can turn into a big black bear."

Viv laughed. "Sounds like fun."

Geoff's wife, Linda, said, "I'll preorder right now."

Mom had disappeared into the kitchen, but I began to

smell something incredible.

"Mom!" I yelled. "Are you making Bananas Foster?"

She poked her head out. "In your honor, prodigal son." She looked at Viv. "Vivienne, round up a couple of the grandkids to help carry to the table and come dish the ice cream for me."

Viv got up and disappeared into the kitchen.

Before any more questions were posed that would require lies for answers, I did a preemptive strike with questions of my own.

"What are you working on right now, Dad?"

He was sitting at the end of the table, still fit with a flat stomach, and tan. I'd heard somebody call him handsome, but I couldn't remember who.

When he smiled, the skin formed crinkles around his eyes. "We're working downtown Mobile. Renovating an old apartment hotel. Turning it into something called a 'boutique' hotel. Irish pub, flower shop, hotel entrance on street level. Rooms above. Stripped it right down to studs so we could rewire, reconfigure the floor plan, and fit with new plumbing. They're calling it Suite Home Alabama."

I chuckled. "Catchy. Wonder where they got that idea? Sounds like the only thing you're keeping is the place on the block."

Dad chuckled. "Pretty much."

Kids were coming in and out delivering bowls of bananas foster which meant that people sitting at the table forgot all about conversation for a few minutes.

"Mom!" I yelled. "This is incredible!"

She came to the kitchen door and took a bow.

As soon as I'd finished with dessert, I got up, carried it into the kitchen and dove into cleanup. There was some resistance since dinner was supposed to be in my honor, but I insisted on doing dishes.

"It's your welcome home dinner. You're not supposed to do dishes."

"I won't take no for an answer," I said. "Let me feel useful."

I did the dishes with two sister-in-laws, kept them talking about their kids, school, soccer, swim team, etc. Since it was a school night, everybody packed up and headed away early leaving me with my mom and dad.

"Y'all are gonna have to forgive me, but I'm turnin' in early."

"Oh, sure. You drove all the way from Los Angeles by yourself. Of course you're tired." Mom gave me a quick hug.

"Yeah. Night."

I had no idea whether I'd driven from Los Angeles or not. And that bothered me. Where had I been and what had I been doing during the last year that had gone missing from memory? Where was I coming from when I 'woke up' on I10?

Shutting the door of my old room, I glanced at the bags sitting on the twin bed across the room from the bed I slept in. I pulled off my boots, stripped down to my boxers, and unzipped the small bag. The book was sitting right on top. I picked it up, turned on the bedside lamp, turned off the overhead light, and crawled into bed.

It was only eight thirty, but I had to escape before I

was forced to tell more lies. Lying to parents had ceased to feel recreational before I turned twenty.

I focused on the book. There had to be a reason why it was the only one I had with me.

The first part was a history of Wimberley. It was reported that it was founded by an English couple about the same time Sam Houston was fighting the Battle of San Jacinto. It was rumored that the husband had been a highwayman in England and that they'd fled with stolen money to a new life one step ahead of the law.

I turned the book over and looked at the cover again. The story seemed so familiar to me, I was thinking I must have read the book before and forgotten about it. Reading on through Deck Durbin's history with the Texas Rangers and Pleasant Wimberley's determination to keep the ranch and tavern going on her own, the story continued to feel overly familiar.

Sometime during the night I woke with the book on my chest and the bedside lamp on. I turned off the light, put the book down, and tried to go back to sleep, but a nagging feeling of emptiness clawed at me, like a hunger that couldn't be satisfied.

THE NEXT MORNING light poured in between the white shutter louvers that covered the windows in my room. I brushed my teeth, threw water in my face and hair, smoothed it into submission, pulled on a pair of jeans and padded into the kitchen.

"There you are beautiful boy," came my mom's cheerful voice. "How about some coffee?"

"Yes," I croaked. "Sorry. Morning voice."

"Sit yourself down right there and let me bring it. I'm not always gonna want to wait on you, but you've been gone a long time and I feel like fussin' over you a little."

I did as I was told and sat down at the big kitchen booth built in the shape of a crescent moon. "Dad already gone?"

"Long time ago. He's still an early riser." She set a cup of coffee in front of me. That was followed by cream and sweeteners. "What are you doing with your day?"

I stared into the cup of coffee. "Not sure. Matter of fact, I was wondering if I can just have a few days to do nothing? I won't stay long. I just need to kind of check out for a little. Would that be okay?"

She scoffed. "Of course, Will. If you're still here in six months, we're going to have a talk, but you're welcome to sanctuary for a few days."

It was such a relief to hear that, it felt like a reprieve. I waited for the brick in my stomach to feel lighter, but nothing happened.

The first day I sat on the side of my bed spinning the black American Express end over end in my hand. When Mom called me for dinner, I said I wasn't feeling up to snuff and asked if I could just eat in my room. She agreed, but looked worried.

The next day I went out, bought myself a laptop at Best Buy, had the geekoids set it up for me, ate tacos at Jack in the Box, and drove home.

I got my folks' wifi password and found out that I could withdraw fifteen thousand dollars in cash before the card expired in fifteen days. But I could buy condos, cars, and all manner of things that could be sold so that I could matriculate through a degree without having to work.

It seemed like a good plan, but I would have to get busy if I wanted to close real estate transactions and buy tons of resalable stuff in two weeks. And that was the rub. I didn't feel motivated to get busy. I didn't feel motivated to do anything except sit in my childhood room and wonder what I'd forgotten.

After four days of this behavior, my mother knocked on my door. I opened it.

"You could use a shave," she said.

I palmed my face and rubbed. "Yeah."

"And you look awful."

"Yeah."

"Come have an iced tea with me."

"Mom…"

"Now."

"Okay."

I trudged behind her to the kitchen. She'd cut a few fresh canna lilies from the garden and set them on the table.

Dutifully, I sat at the table and waited. She set an ice tea in front of me.

"What's the problem, Will? You've spent four days in your room doing something that looks a lot like hiding. You're thirty. Too old for that nonsense. What's going on?"

There were only two choices. Lie or tell the truth. If I lied, she'd know. If I told the truth, she might think I'm crazy.

"Heart to heart? If I tell you the truth, it has to be confidential. You have to promise."

"You know I'm good at keepin' stuff to myself when I want to. What's the problem?"

"It's big."

She blew out a breath. "Am I going to need an Arnold Lit?"

"It's ten in the morning."

"Answer the question."

"Maybe."

She got up, and set an ice tea glass on the counter. She pulled the gallon jar of sweet tea out of the fridge and poured until the glass was a third full. She then pulled out the gallon jar of lemonade and filled the glass another third full. Stepping out the back door, she pulled a sprig of mint from the plants she kept by the back steps, ran tap water over it and threw it in the glass. Next went in enough ice cubes to fill it almost all the way up. The last step was the part that caused my mother to rename her favorite concoction Arnold 'Lit'. She added three 'splashes' of vodka to the Arnold Palmer and stirred. Satisfied that she was ready for anything, she sat down again.

"Okay. Hit me," she said.

I blew out a breath. "Okay. Here goes. I don't know any other way to explain this. I woke up behind the wheel of that car to find that I was being pulled over by highway patrol on I10 the other side of Houston. He said I was doing eighty seven in a seventy five. Anyway, disoriented doesn't begin to cover it. I thought he was gonna say it was grand theft auto. 'Cause I have no idea where that car came from or how or why I was heading east on I10 with a black American Express card and six pairs of cowboy boots."

The smile left my mother's face. I had her one hundred percent attention. She took a drink of Arnold Lit without taking her eyes away from me.

"He asked me for proof of insurance and my driver's license. What I pulled out of my wallet was an Alabama license with this address on it. Same for insurance. My name. This address. So he gave me a speeding ticket and let me go. I don't have to tell you that doesn't make any sense because I haven't used this address for more than a decade."

I took a drink of tea and a deep breath before continuing.

"So I have five thousand dollars cash in my wallet in addition to the black American Express card that expires the end of this month. In ten days. I have no idea where any of that came from either. What's more? I've lost a whole year. Last thing I remember I was planning to quit acting and come home, but that was October of *last* year."

"Do you think you're mixed up in organized crime? Drugs?"

There was a stack of cold biscuits sitting on a plate. I grabbed one and took a bite out of it more because of nervousness than being hungry.

I raised my hands. "How do I know? I can't say no because I just don't know." And the Voice was being obstinately silent. Deadly silent. "That's not the worst of it.

The worst of it is that I feel like I've done something horrible, something wrong. As in *really* wrong. I just don't know what it is. I've lost something I need. Something I don't think I can live without. And I don't know what it is."

She stared at me a long time.

"Say something," I finally said.

She stood and put her hand to my forehead like she was checking for a fever.

"I'm not running a temperature, Mom."

"I didn't think you were. That's not what I'm checking for."

"Well, what...?"

"What else?" She sat down again. "Have you left anything out?"

I thought about it. "Like what?"

"Visions? Strange feelings about things?"

"Visions?" Like the woman in the car? "Well, when I was driving Pass Christian by the water, for a second I thought I saw a woman in the car with me. Long black hair. I didn't see her face. It was just for a second."

She nodded. "What else?"

"There was a book in my luggage and, speaking of that, the first time I've seen those clothes was last night when I stopped at a hotel and opened those bags. I've got seven pairs of cowboy boots. Apparently I love them. When the hell did that happen? And how?"

"What's the book?"

"It's about a ghost, of all things. I started reading it last night. I have a strong feeling that I've read it before or know the story somehow."

"Show me."

I got up, retrieved the book, and set it down on the kitchen table. She made a face. "Wimberley, huh? Figures."

"What? What figures?"

"I'm gonna take you to see somebody."

I slumped down in my chair. "You think I'm crazy."

She frowned. "No. Not that kinda somebody. But you're gonna have to turn loose of some of that green in your wallet, because she ain't cheap."

"So you don't think I'm crazy."

"I don't think you're crazy."

I took a minute to absorb that. After hearing my story, my mother came to the conclusion that I'm not crazy. "Who is it you're taking me to see?"

She shook her head. "Just trust me. We'll get to the bottom of this. Let me ask you something. Do you remember calling just about this time last year? I remember it was late October because I was putting out gourds and mums on the front porch in between trying to control your dad's mad gardening ideas."

I was shaking my head. "No. I don't remember that."

"You told me you had a live-in girlfriend."

"I did?"

"Wow. That doesn't sound like me. What else did I say?"

"That her name was Rave. That you were moving to Wimberley, Texas and going back to school. Does that jog any memories?"

I grabbed my head. "It doesn't jog memories, exactly,

but something you said just gave me one hell of a piercing headache. And maybe heartburn, too." I squinted at her between my fingers. "What else?"

"I haven't talked to you since then. Whenever I tried to call, I just got static. Couldn't even leave a message. Sent a lot of texts, but they were never delivered. Failed to send."

"Wow."

"You're repeating yourself." She rose. "Just relax. Have some breakfast. Watch some TV. Let me see what I can set up."

"Okay."

Fifteen minutes later she came back in the kitchen. "Go get ready. We have an appointment in two hours and it's an hour and a half journey from here."

I didn't question her further. I showered, shaved, pulled on a pair of jeans and tee so soft they were as comfortable as pajamas, picked a pair of brown snakeskin boots and I was ready to go. I made the bed, put my wallet and phone in my pockets, and grabbed the car keys.

"You want to take my car?"

Mom grinned. "Don't be silly. You think I get the chance to ride in a car like that every day? Of course we're taking your car."

I smiled at her. "You navigate."

"You're in good hands."

"Where we goin'?"

"I know somebody who lives on a little island off Heron Bay. Don't worry. You'll like her. Probably. You got cash?"

"Yes. I heard you say green."

She nodded. "Just bring that and an *open* mind. You'll be fine."

THE RAG TOP stayed on the Boxster because of a probability of rain. It was just as well. My mother probably didn't want to get blown around for a couple of hours, although it was hard to predict with her.

When we got to Heron Bay, she directed me to a tiny marina then walked into the office like she owned the place. "We need a ride over to the island and back. Means waitin' around a couple of hours or so. How much for that?"

An old guy with white hair and beard sat behind stacks of papers including mail that probably hadn't been opened for years.

"Well," he said, "I might have somebody who could take you over." He rubbed his beard, looked my mother over, did the same with me, and when his eyes got to the boots I knew we were screwed. He looked from the boots up at me with a smile that said he'd taken my rich boy measure.

"Think four hundred is fair."

"You providing a five course gourmet dinner with that?"

The guy's smile fell. "Time's worth something, missy."

I didn't like hearing my mother called 'missy'. It sounded all kinds of wrong. I started to step forward, but she put a hand on my arm. "Two hundred and a fifty dollar tip if the driver is nice and I don't get sprayed on the way over."

"Three hundred."

"One seventy five."

The old guy narrowed his eyes. "Two hundred, a fifty dollar tip for Stevie, and a fifty dollar tip for me."

When Mom looked at me, I nodded.

"Done," she said.

Crusty guy held out his hand until I put two hundred dollar bills on his palm. Then he picked up the phone. After a few seconds he said, "Got a job for ya." He hung up, apparently without waiting for an answer.

A few minutes later we heard steps on the decking outside the office. A kid entered and nodded at us. He was fairly ordinary looking. About twenty years old, with lanky hair that hung around his ears.

"This is Stevie," old guy said. "He'll take ya."

To Stevie, he said, "Take 'em over to the island and wait for the roundtrip. Grab a sandwich, some water, magazine, whatever."

Stevie opened the small refrigerator and withdrew a couple of bottled waters and one of those packaged sandwiches that you get in convenience stores, the ones with bread so soggy it's falling apart because of the lettuce and tomato. Ugh.

"This way," he said.

We followed him for a short walk down the pier. He stopped at a small motorboat. Frankly, for three hundred dollars I had thought we might have bought something bigger, but I wasn't in a position to argue.

While Stevie untied, I stepped into the boat and then

helped Mom.

"Mom," I said under my breath. "Have you been to this place before?"

"Oh, sure," she said. "Lots of times."

Well, that was a surprise.

AS WE NEARED the island, Mom directed Stevie to a private dock with easy access pier and steps.

"We'll be back in about two hours," she told Stevie. He nodded and went about tying off.

I followed her up a crushed granite path lined with overarching trees that ended in a magnificent semitropical garden. The house beyond was a one story yellow clapboard with white shutters and porches all around. The word that came to mind was inviting.

It had just begun to drizzle when we reached the front door. I hoped Stevie had a pancho.

My mother walked right in without knocking.

"Mistral!" she yelled. "We're here!"

I heard a voice from somewhere deeper in the house. When the woman emerged I saw that she was about the same age as my mother and shared Mom's penchant for bright-colored clothing. Her hair was highlighted with streaks of light blonde that complimented her tan and sky blue eyes. She was really attractive for a hermit.

"Katrina," she grinned at Mom. "It's nice to see you." After giving Mom a hug, her eyes wandered to me. "Who's this?"

"My baby, Willem."

"Willem," she rolled it on her tongue. "I like it." She

looked me over. "Have a problem, do we?"

She cocked her head like she was evaluating. I didn't want to say something smart ass like, "Duh. That's why we're here." So I remained quiet and let her answer her rhetorical question herself.

"Let's get some refreshments and sit on the back porch. I love to be out on the porch when it's raining."

"That sounds perfect, Mistral," said Mom.

We followed her through the house and found that she had already set a table with petit fours, little sandwich squares, and what appeared to be an iced pitcher of Arnold Palmers, complete with the same mint my mother used.

"This is beautiful, isn't it, Willem? Thank you for going to so much trouble for us."

"No trouble at all, Katrina. It's always lovely to have you."

After she poured drinks and encouraged us to help ourselves to the tea goodies, she turned to me and said, "Willem, do you mind if I touch you?"

"Actually I prefer Will. And it depends on where."

She laughed. "Very well, Will. I have no interest in becoming overly personal with you. After all, you're the child of a friend."

I glanced at my mother. She hadn't used the word 'friend', although it was clear they enjoyed a familiar relationship.

"Sure. Go ahead."

Oddly, she got up and put her hand on my forehead exactly as my mother had done.

"Hmmm," she said as she returned to her seat. "You've been enchanted."

My mouth fell open. "What does that mean?"

"Enchanted?" She raised both eyebrows like she thought I might be dense. "Bespelled. Bewitched. Ensorceled. Enthralled. Hexed. Fucked with. Understand?"

I frowned. "I understand that last one."

"Where has he been?" she asked my mother.

Mom rolled her eyes and said, "Wimberley."

Mistral looked back at me. "Of course. How long were you there, Will?"

I looked at my mother, who answered for me like I was a child. "Possibly a year."

Not willing to be left out of the conversation, I jumped in. "What do you know about Wimberley? And what did you mean by 'of course'?"

"My great-grandmother used to live there. She was asked to leave. Apparently she didn't fit in. Will, tell me in your own words what the problem is."

"I've lost a year, meaning I don't remember anything that's happened since October of *last* year!"

She waved a hand around. "Yes. Yes. I know. But that's not really a problem. What's bothering you?"

She didn't think losing a year was a big deal?

"Search your heart. Tell me what's *really* bothering you."

Search my heart?

"I feel like I've done something really bad, something I regret, but I don't know what it is. Something's missing. Something I think I can't live without."

"Well put. The spell you're wearing is like a film covering your memories. It's pressed and sealed into place kind of like the plastic wrap you put over leftovers. It can be lifted away if that's what you want."

I sat up straighter. "Yes. That's what I want!"

As soon as I said it, I wondered where my healthy dose of skepticism was. I was missing a year. This stranger said I'd been enchanted and I was going along with that diagnosis as if it was unquestionably true. On the other hand, I didn't have anything to lose, besides a few bucks.

"You're incredibly lucky that you have a mother who can recognize symptoms and that she knows somebody who can correct such things."

I looked at Mom with a newfound respect.

"Alright. I'm not going to pull punches," Mistral said. "Sometimes this is painful."

I nodded. "So is not knowing what's going on."

"Katrina," she said to Mom, "maybe you'd like to go inside. This could be hard for you to watch."

Mom brought herself up to her full height. "I'll stay. I won't interfere."

"See that you don't," warned Mistral.

"You ready?" she asked. When I nodded, she said, "Close your eyes."

The minute I did I felt like my insides were being vacuumed. I gasped and tried to open my eyes, but they stayed closed. I tried to stand, but I couldn't move. Then wave after wave of memory was restored. Orientation. The contest. Destiny and her beagle. Turning Raider over in the river. The Witches' Ball. My beautiful Ravish. Our life together. School. Friends. Singing to Rave. And finally, the look of betrayal on her face when I told her I wasn't staying.

I doubled over and began dry-heaving, struggling to get breath into my lungs in between gags.

"What you're experiencing is perfectly normal," Mistral said. "Just relax into it and it will pass shortly. You're going to be fine."

Slowly the impulse to gag began to subside as did the inability to get enough air into my lungs. When I was able to open my eyes, I sat up, still panting. My eyes were watering. She handed me a tissue and I took it.

"Wow," I said, wiping my eyes. "Are you one of them?"

Mistral smiled. "What's in a name? I can't sing and I can't ski worth beans. But I can do this."

"Yeah," I said. "Good job. What do I owe you?"

"Two thousand."

Truthfully, I wouldn't have questioned it if she'd said more. After all, how much was it worth for me to find out why I couldn't get comfortable inside my own body. She was right. I was lucky that Mom was Mom.

I pulled out my wallet, counted out twenty bills, and put it back in my pocket.

"So," Mistral said, "you love her?"

I thought about that for a few seconds and found that I was grinning. "Yeah. I guess I do. What a shame I had to put her through this to figure out that I'm a douche."

"Well, Willem Wizard, I'm betting the colony is going to be real glad to see you heading back their way. You carry the promise of strong witchy daughters."

I just stared at her.

Willem Wizard?

Mom was shaking her head. "He doesn't know there's a strain running through the family."

Mistral looked surprised. "Oh. Well, now you do. It's strong on your mother's side and you got some from your dad as well. Your name, Draiocht, means wizard."

"I didn't know that."

"Have something to eat before you go. There's not a decent restaurant between here and Mobile."

I took a couple of the dainty little sandwiches and washed them down with a gulp of minty Arnold. I grabbed a handful of little sweets on our way out and ate them on the path back to the boat.

I looked at my watch. "We were there for an hour and a half?"

"Yeah. It was worth it though. Right?"

"Mom, you're incredible. How did you know what was wrong and who could fix it?"

"Well, over the years there have been things that needed a little help from outside, a slight course correction you might say. I'm a client of Mistral's."

"And you knew this was a magical problem?"

"Like she said, there's a little bit of the gift running through your own family. That's probably why the memory wipe didn't work as well on you as it does on some people."

"I have to get back. I still have nine days to make this right."

"Or you turn into a pumpkin?"

"Pretty much. I have to get Rave to take me back before the clock strikes midnight on All Hallows."

"Okay. So you're leaving in the morning?"

"No. Leaving as soon as we get back." I was feeling giddy with hope. "This ride has satellite, Mom. See if you can find us some road trip music."

Within a couple of minutes we were speeding along, listening to Alabama Shakes. I was feeling lighthearted as possible for a man who knew he had to face his woman and grovel, crawl if necessary, anything to have her turn a smile my way again.

chapter eleven

IT WAS FOUR o'clock by the time I had luggage back in the car trunk and was standing on the driveway giving my mom a hug.

"You're getting one hell of a Mothers' Day present next May," I said. "You may have saved my life."

"That's what mothers are for. No thanks necessary, but I wouldn't mind a car like the one you're driving."

After one last kiss on the cheek, I jumped in the car and pulled away as she waved goodbye. "Tell Dad I said I'll be back soon and we'll catch up then. I hope you can figure out something to say to him so that he doesn't think…"

"No worries. Anyway, you know your dad. He's not big on judging."

I pulled up to the Four Seasons around eleven o'clock and was recognized since I'd just been there a couple of days before. My plan was to get a few hours' sleep, have a big breakfast at the hotel, and be in Wimberley by ten. I didn't count on being so excited that sleep eluded me, but I dozed enough to drive safe.

The next morning I had steak and eggs, hash browns, fruit and coffee. I was ready for bear. Thought about Izzy when I had that thought and smiled. I couldn't wait to get back to Wimberley and start trying to set things right. I knew I'd hurt Rave, foolishly, needlessly, but I just had to believe I could persuade her to take me back. And if I could, I'd spend the rest of my life showering her with reasons to be glad she gave me another chance.

What I wouldn't give to have listened to Deck Derbin.

He was right. Hell means having to live without the woman you love.

I BREEZED STRAIGHT through town on a mission to get to the colony as soon as possible. It was mid-morning when I pulled up to the gates. Someone had forgotten to remove the auto gate opener from the car because it swung inward on my approach. That was a lucky break. Apparently nobody told the guard not to let me in either. He waved as I went through.

In two minutes I was parked in front of our house. Or rather, what was left of our house. There was no front door. The windows were all blown out. The columns were gone and the pristine white walls were covered with soot and ash. It had burned and, from the look of it, it wasn't a small fire.

I was sitting on the hood of the car staring at the ruin, thinking that Rave must have been devastated to the core to destroy the house she loved, when I heard the rumble of a motorcycle. Raider pulled in front of me. He killed his motor, but didn't get off his bike. His face looked completely impassive.

"What're you doing here, Will?"

"I live here, Raider."

"Not anymore."

"That's not what my contract says. My contract says I'm promised to Ravish Wimberley for a year and a day. That's eight more days. What happened here?"

"Guess."

"She burned the place down."

"How is it you're here? How is it you remember?"

I swung my gaze from the ruin of my house to Raider. "True love."

He barked out a scoffing laugh. "When you walked away, it didn't look much like true love to me."

"That's because I was blinded by idiocy. Now I'm not. And I'm back. To stay."

"To stay," he repeated flatly.

"What makes you think she'd want you back?"

"If she's feeling the way I'm feeling, she'll find a way to forgive me."

"What if she's not feeling the way you're feeling?"

"Then I'm doomed. Where is she?"

"Camping. On the preserve. I don't know exactly where." His eyes drifted to the Boxster. "She's in rugged territory. You're not going to find her in that car."

After considering the wisdom of that, I said, "What do you suggest?"

"Why should I want to help you?"

"I saved your life."

That got me the faintest ghost of a smile. "There's a Jeep dealership in San Marcos. It's only twenty minutes away."

"Come on. Leave the car. I'll give you a ride."

"Ride bitch holding on to your ugly carcass? For twenty whole minutes?"

"You want your woman back or not?"

I hopped off the hood. "Let's go."

"I'm givin' you a head start here. If Rave's family finds out you're back before she can protect you, you could end up one of those flat iron frogs on the highway."

"Thanks. I'll owe you one."

"You're also gonna need some serious hardware to break the lock on the preserve gate."

"Okay."

"I'll get that while you're horse tradin' at the dealership."

I nodded. "Thanks, again, Raider. You're a good friend."

"Yeah? Well, try not to forget it so easy again, hero."

TWENTY FIVE MINUTES later I was standing in the Jeep dealership in San Marcos telling them I needed to walk away with something in stock. They had a seventy-fifth anniversary limited edition 4x4 with every imaginable bell and whistle. It was a gorgeous deep maroon and I knew on sight that Rave would love it.

I paid with my black American Express that still had nine days to expiration and waited in the parking lot for Raider to return with a lock buster. He stopped next to me, pulled the monstrous thing out of his saddlebag, and said. "Good luck."

"Thanks. This was a good suggestion. She's gonna love

this car."

He gave a little salute and headed back to Wimberley with a wide arc U turn.

I stopped by the florist for a purple orchid then stopped by the convenience store for a Styrofoam cooler, ice, and Rave's favorite wine coolers. I thought it would be a good idea to show up with something more romantic than just a new Jeep.

An hour and a half later I'd found her campsite, but not her. I was parked and waiting. When she hadn't shown up after five hours, I plundered her camp to find a protein bar. I was in the middle of scarfing it down when she pulled up in a Jeep that was so caked with thick mud it would have been impossible to tell what color it was underneath. But the top was down.

She stopped the car next to me.

"You break the lock?" she asked. Her expression was set, her eyes were hard.

"Yes," I said.

"You steal my protein bar?"

"Yes," I answered. I stepped over to the shiny new Jeep. "But I brought you a new car." I reached into the passenger side and came up with a purple orchid. "And this."

She looked the Jeep over. "It's nice."

"I also brought your fav wine coolers."

"What are you doing here, Will?"

"Asking you to take me back."

Her eyes widened. "How do you even remember? Harmony wiped you."

I took a step toward her, but sidestepped the question. "I remember everything including the fact that I'm an asshole."

She raised her chin. "You are." She agreed. "If that's an apology, then I accept. Now take your wine coolers and go."

"Can't."

"Can't what?"

"Can't go."

"Why not?"

"Well, two reasons. First, I love you. Second, I'm under contract until All Hallows." I locked her eyes to mine and said, "As. Are. You."

"So what?"

"On November first, I plan to renew. Forever."

"It's too late for that, Will. You don't believe in love. Remember?"

"That was idiot Will. Idiot Will is dead. The Will who knows what's good for him knows he can't live without you. And this Will definitely believes in love."

She stared for so long I was starting to squirm like a worm underneath her gaze.

"I can't just switch my emotions on again and off again, Will. You hurt me."

I took another step toward her. "Let me make it up to you."

"How are you going to do that?"

"You can tie me to the bed and tickle me with feathers?"

The line between her brows smoothed out and I saw

the tiniest smile playing on her beautiful lips.

"I can't make you go away because you're right. You do still have a contract. I don't know how you managed to remember that, but I don't have to love you or take care of you."

"See. Here's the thing I found out about love. You don't get to decide whether you do or you don't. Love decides for you. You don't have to love me, but you do." She looked away. "I'm so sorry I hurt you, Rave. Sorry I hurt us both, but I'm really sorry for causing you pain. If I could undo it, I would. If you take me back, I promise to spend the rest of my life making it up to you."

"That's an awful big promise."

"I've got an awful big feeling for you." I took another step toward her, which brought me within arm's length. "I saw the house. It made my heart hurt."

She looked down and sniffed. "You made me cry."

"I know." I closed the distance between us and she let me put my arms around her. "You didn't deserve that. What you deserve is adoration." I kissed her cheeks and her chin and her forehead, wiped away the single tear that trailed down her face. "You know how I know you love me?"

"How?"

"Glory told me I was leaving with five thousand dollars, my clothes, and a car. She didn't say anything about a black American Express card."

Rave turned her head. "I wanted to make sure you were taken care of."

I smiled. "I feel taken care of right now, with you

pressed close to me." I felt her body relax against me. "So. We're living in a tent?"

"I didn't agree to live anywhere with you."

"Okay. I'll sleep outside the tent then."

"It's going to rain."

"How do you know?"

"Because if you sleep outside the tent I'm going to ask Deli to make it rain."

"Really? I'd better go back to town and get some plastic garbage bags."

"Do what you want."

She put the Jeep in reverse and left me standing there holding an orchid.

I drove into town and bought a box of garbage bags and a bucket of fried chicken. When she came back at sundown, I was sitting on garbage bags eating a wing.

"What are you doing?"

"Sitting outside the tent eating chicken."

"You're not really going to sleep outside the tent."

"Yes. I am. I'm going to be as close to you as you will allow."

She cocked her head and looked at the bucket. "Can I have a breast?"

I looked inside the round carton to see what was left. "I might have one. Extra crispy. You can have it if you let me come inside the tent." She blinked slowly. "With you."

"You can't come inside the tent with me."

"Well, what are you offering then?"

"I can put the house back together."

I leaned back and looked into her face. "You can?"

"Are you staying?"

"Until one of us passes from this life, I'm here. I'm yours. Completely."

"You can't sleep with me until after you make it real. If you sign the forever contract. Until then you have to stay in the guest room."

"Whatever you say."

She searched my face for a full minute. When she was satisfied with what she saw, she said, "Let's go home."

She pulled out her phone and made a call. I heard her say, "Come back to work."

I helped her take down the campsite and stow everything in the muddy Jeep.

While we were working, I said, "Can I sign the permanent contract now?"

She smiled. "Now you're in a hurry?"

"Well, yeah." I smiled. "I have several powerful motivations."

"Not until All Hallows."

I groaned. "What about kissing?"

She was silent for a long time. "Maybe. We'll see."

I gave her the keys to the new Jeep and followed her back to the colony in the one that was so covered with mud I could barely see out the windshield.

The Boxster was still sitting on the street in front of our house, only the house was completely restored to its former beauty. A year ago I would have said such a thing was impossible, but that was before I learned what it meant to be consort to a Wimberley witch.

She parked the new Jeep in the garage and I left the

muddy one out on the driveway. Ed could deal with it later.

"How did you manage to be here with two cars?" she asked.

"Raider gave me a ride to San Marcos to buy you a new Jeep."

"Raider," she said shaking her head.

She pulled out her phone and made another call. "I'm home. Will is back. He's staying. Let everybody know." Pause. "I'm not sure, but it doesn't matter. What does matter is that we're having a party the last day of this month." Pause. "Okay. Call Mom first. Bye."

I walked around the end of the Jeep and allowed her to kiss me stupid.

"Welcome home." She smiled.

I rested my forehead against hers. "This is home. Right here."

She put her finger to my lips. "Where's my chicken breast?"

"Safe and sound."

"I'm eating. Then I'm taking a bath. I've been camping for days."

I SAT ON the floor next to the tub where Ravish was soaking. It was pure torture, but when it comes to my prize, I'm a glutton for punishment.

I said, "What do you think happens after we die?"

"I think our spirits go to Summerland."

"What if spirits don't leave?"

"It's unfortunate, but it happens sometimes."

"Is there any way to, I don't know, help a spirit leave? I've read about it being done."

"Yes. Sometimes. Prissy might be able to do it. Why?"

"Deck Durbin's ghost. He tried really hard to stop me from leaving. As part of making amends, I'd like to help him move on. I think what he wants is to be where Pleasant is. He says hell is living without her, knowing he'll never see her again."

She smiled. "That's pretty romantic, Will."

I shrugged. "I just know how it feels to be separated from the person you love. I can't imagine being in that state for centuries."

She splashed water on her throat and said, "Okay. I'll call her. Leave so I can get out of the tub."

"No."

"What do you mean no?"

"You said no sleeping with you until the forever ceremony. You didn't say no looking." She laughed. "You also didn't say no fucking."

"So you're a lawyer now?"

I shook my head. "No. Just a very horny guy who's desperately in love with you."

"You're really staying?"

"Till death and even then I hope we're not parted."

She grabbed my shirt and pulled me into the tub with her where she proceeded to make major compromises on what constituted 'sleeping' before All Hallows.

On October thirty-first, we had a party at our house for close friends and family. I swore on my honor, my soul, and my love for Ravish, that wild horses and mad demons could not drag me away from her again. Not in this life or the next. I give thanks every day that she believed me.

EPILOGUE

THE FIRST TIME Simon saw me after I came back he punched me in the face. He didn't break my nose, but he did split my lip. I hadn't realized our friendship meant so much to him.

THE RITUAL TO send Derbin's ghost to the hereafter became a community-wide event. Not everybody could see him, but those of us who could agreed that he left smiling.

AS FOR ME, I was a very enthusiastic participant in the next year's Orientation video. I finished my degree at U.T. Now I do guest lectures on paranormal studies.

A few years later I became mayor of Wimberley. You might say I'm the colony's most devoted resident. I spend every day trying to make sure that Rave never regrets giving me another chance.

Among other things, I changed my mind about children. We have a beautiful daughter named Mistral and another on the way. Who knew that the sexiest thing in the world is seeing your woman's belly swell with your progeny? Damn. We may have a big, big family.

YES. WE VISIT Fairhope a couple of times a year.

Yes. My mother got a Porsche Spyder Boxster for Mother's Day, custom painted her signature turquoise. She's the best. The very best.

ALSO BY VICTORIA DANANN

Knights of Black Swan 1, My Familiar Stranger

Knights of Black Swan 2, The Witch's Dream

Knights of Black Swan 3, A Summoner's Tale

Knights of Black Swan 4, Moonlight

Knights of Black Swan 5, Gathering Storm

Knights of Black Swan 6, A Tale of Two Kingdoms

Knights of Black Swan 7, Solomon's Sieve

An Order of the Black Swan Novel, Prince of Demons

Knights of Black Swan 8, Vampire Hunter

Knights of Black Swan 9, Journey Man

Knights of Black Swan 10 (2016)

THE HYBRIDS
Exiled 1. CARNAL

Exiled 2. CRAVE

Exiled 3, CHARMING (July 2016)

THE WEREWOLVES
New Scotia Pack 1, Shield Wolf: Liulf

New Scotia Pack 2, Wolf Lover: Konochur

New Scotia Pack 3, Cinead, Born of Fire (2016)

THE WITCHES OF WIMBERLEY

Witches of Wimberley 1; Willem

Witches of Wimberley 1; Wednesday

Witches of Wimberley 1; Wick

CONTEMPORARY ROMANCE

Sons of Sanctuary MC, Book 1. Two Princes

Sons of Sanctuary MC, Book 2. The Biker's Brother

Links to all Victoria's books can be found here...

www.VictoriaDanann.com

Victoria Danann

NEW YORK TIMES and USA TODAY
BESTSELLING AUTHOR

SUBSCRIBE TO MY MAIL LIST Be first to know…
http://eepurl.com/wRE3T

Victoria's Website
victoriadanann.com

Victoria's Facebook Page
facebook.com/victoriadanannbooks

Victoria's Facebook Fan Group
facebook.com/groups/772083312865721

Twitter
twitter.com/vdanann

Pinterest
pinterest.com/vdanann

Made in the USA
San Bernardino, CA
14 February 2020

64431939R00157